Willow Place Revisited

Joan Clinton Scoggins

Joan Scoggins
306 Warthen St.
La Fayette, GA 30728-2529

Willow Place Revisited

THE SEQUEL TO WILLOW PLACE

JOAN CLINTON SCOGGINS

Pleasant W rd

Dedication

. . . To my husband, Max and our sons Phillip Anthony and Gregory Norman.
With all my love.

. . . To my eternal friend Jane Crawford Collett.

. . . Also to every person who read my first book "*Willow Place*", you have my heart felt thanks.

Foreword

The writing of any book has its inspiration and purpose. For the last year the inspiration I have received from my readers of *"Willow Place"*, their comments, support, and sincerely expressed appreciation for the journey to *"Willow Place"*, has generated another chapter in the lives of its characters.

Coupled with the readers expressed eagerness to continue their journey, I sincerely hope that blessings of love, joy, and anticipation will flow from its pages.

Over fifty years ago, God placed the desire in my heart to pen my thoughts and feelings of His inspiration to others through me. Because of this profound desire, the concept of writing my first book *"Willow Place"* began to grow as the seed of a willow tree. That desire was fulfilled and today the story expands to my readers as "Willow Place" is revisited.

What stories of love, Godliness, inspiration, and intrigue will emerge? The answers lie within the following pages.

Chapter 1

April 1869

*T*he sound of gunfire startled Elizabeth out of a deep sleep. She sat upright in bed and realized she was only dreaming. The hateful Civil War had tortured many a night's sleep for her.

The early morning sun had begun to dimly light the bedroom. The draperies had been left open the night before. She and Zachary agreed that the beauty of the full moon was just too pretty to be shut out.

Elizabeth looked at the face of her beloved husband as he slept. His breathing was rhythmic, signaling a restful sleep. His bare broad shoulders were marred by a scar from a gunshot wound suffered in the Battle of Richmond near the end of the war.

Tender emotions within her heart surfaced as she felt his nearness. She cherished the gift of love they shared. As she quietly eased back down on her side watching him sleep, Elizabeth let her mind wander back in time.

It was twelve years ago this month Zachary and her Grandfather Morgan had gone to New York on a buying trip for their carriage company. It was the first time since their marriage that Elizabeth and Zachary had been apart. Before he left she had not told him they were expecting their first child. The anticipation of sharing this news with him when he returned the next day filled her with joy.

She remembered she was sitting on the balcony thinking about their life together when she saw Mark from the telegraph office riding swiftly toward Willow Place. She rushed downstairs to the front door. Mr. Ferris told Mark not to waste any time delivering the telegram. Elizabeth was terrified at the thought of reading the message for fear of what it might say. She well remembered the telegram she had received twelve years earlier saying that Zachary and Ben were lost at sea. That message paralyzed her with fear. It was two long days before she learned they had made it to safety. However, this time, the fear in her heart was all for naught. Indeed, the telegram contained good news.

On the buying trip to New York, Zachary and her Grandfather Morgan had met some businessmen who were very interested in marketing their newly designed MBH Carriage. These men wanted Morgan Carriage Company to open a carriage factory in Philadelphia. They owned some property there and felt it would be an ideal location for a new factory. Zachary and John wanted Elizabeth and Catherine to meet them in New York the next day. They needed at least another week to discuss the possibility of this venture. The telegram read:

Elizabeth and Catherine, please join us in New York tomorrow. Will meet you at the train depot at 6:00 p.m. Good news about our carriage company. Will explain. Love, Zachary

Elizabeth remembered the relief and then the excitement. She and her Grandmother Catherine were like schoolgirls packing for the trip and even enjoying the long train ride from Richmond to New York.

Elizabeth and her grandmother shopped in the daytime while Zachary and her grandfather met with their prospective partners. They had delightful evening meals at some of the best restaurants in New York and attended two concerts and a stage production. The businessmen orchestrated these events for the four of them. Morgan Carriage Company of Philadelphia was opened for business six months later and had been a very gainful business venture . . . until the Civil War. They lost the entire company.

Chapter 2

Zachary stirred, opened his eyes and exclaimed, "Don't you have something better to do than watch me sleep?" Then he kissed her on the forehead and asked, "What were you thinking about?"

"Oh, just about that good looking man I met at the train depot here in Richmond, the one who completely stole my heart. Did I ever tell you about him?" Elizabeth asked with a twinkle in her eye.

"Only about a million times," Zachary replied. "By the way, what ever happened to him?"

"He's still around. Comes to see me from time to time. Sometimes brings me flowers. Are you jealous?"

"Me jealous? Heavens no! Remember, I get to enjoy the flowers, too."

With that, Zachary swept Elizabeth up in his arms and carried her to the door of the balcony, swung it open, and stepped out into the bright morning sunshine. She snuggled close to him feeling the strength of his arms around her. What a safe place to be this beautiful April morning.

Later, sitting at the breakfast table, Elizabeth looked first at Morgan and then at Savannah. Where had the years gone? Morgan would be twelve years old on November 24th. And Savannah would be ten on September 19th. Morgan had Elizabeth's black hair but also had many of the features of his father, while Savannah had her father's blonde hair and Elizabeth's features. What a joy these two had been to them.

Morgan was serious-minded and very interested in his studies. He was tall for his age, lean, and muscular from the hard work he did around Willow Place. He spent as much time as possible working with the horses, gathering hay and doing other chores that always had to be done. He had a thirst for learning, both in the classroom as well as outside interests. Morgan was not a person of indecision. He always knew his own mind and was adventurous in nature.

Savannah was a real charmer and curious about everything. She was relentless with her questions until she got an answer that satisfied her curiosity. Riding over Willow Place exploring every pig trail was her delight. This place was her haven. She declared she would never leave Willow Place! Savannah had her father wrapped around her little finger. He corrected her, for her own good, but never in anger. Zachary adored this little replica of her mother.

Elizabeth thought to herself . . . *what a pleasure these two children are to me. Our life has been so fulfilled in raising them. I can't imagine our lives before they came. Lord, help me never to do anything that would bring a reproach to our family name, a reproach they would also have to bear. I want them to be proud to tell anyone who their mother and father are.*

Rosie had packed Zachary, Morgan and Savannah's lunches and was shooing them out the door. George, their carriage driver, would take the children to school and Zachary on to the carriage company.

"Rosie Gilbert, it was our lucky day when you came into our lives a short while after the war ended. I don't know what would become of this family if it weren't for you!" Elizabeth said emphatically.

"I'm inclined to agree with you," Rosie retorted. "It takes a firm hand to keep this family on track. I hope I'm able to look after you for a long time to come."

Chapter 3

*S*omehow, Elizabeth was in a very nostalgic mood this morning. She carried a fresh cup of coffee to the library and sat down at her Grandfather Baldwin's big oak desk. She reached toward the bookcase behind her and took one of her many journals and began to read. The entry read:

> . . . April 23, 1857: Zachary and grandfather have been gone a week to New York on a buying trip. They are due back tomorrow. It's the first time we've been apart since we were married last November 16th. I miss Zachary terribly. I'll never get used to his being away. I've some interesting news for him when he returns. It'll change our lives forever . . .

Elizabeth looked up from the journal and glanced out the window toward the lake and those gorgeous Willow trees. She shuddered, remembering the day she received Zachary's telegram with good news when she feared so it would contain something bad. She scolded herself again for thinking the worst instead of the best. There was a note made in the margin of her journal quoting one of Zachary's favorite scriptures: Philippians 4:7 and 8 . . . "And the peace of God, which passeth all understanding, shall keep your hearts and minds through Christ Jesus. Finally, brethren, whatsoever things are true, whatsoever things are honest, whatsoever things are just, whatsoever things are pure, whatsoever things are lovely, whatsoever things are of good report: think on these things." Zachary told her if she would put this scripture into practice, it would spare her a lot of anguish.

Then she read her entry a week after Morgan Thomas Bainbridge was born:

> . . . A week ago, on November 24, 1857, a tiny miracle came to live with us at Willow Place. He weighed seven pounds and looks exactly like his father except his hair is black, just like mine. Zachary and I prayed a prayer of dedication to teach Morgan, just like my Grandfather Baldwin taught me, according to Deuteronomy 6: 5–7 . . .

Still thinking nostalgically, she chose another of her journals and turned to the week after Savannah Jane Bainbridge was born. The entry read:

> . . . On September 19, 1859 God blessed us with a daughter whom we have named Savannah Jane; Savannah for my grandmother, and Jane is Zachary's mother's middle name. She is perfect. She weighed seven pounds, just like her brother, Morgan. Zachary says she looks like me except for her hair that is colored like her father's. She even has my dimples. We are dedicating her to the Lord just as we did Morgan . . .

After Savannah was born, Elizabeth stopped making daily entries in her journal. These two precious babies took up most of her time.

Chapter 4

The Civil War broke out in 1861. She resumed her daily writing. The war was devastating both to the South and North. She felt she must make some entries in her journal each day, even if only a few lines. She remembered the frenzy that prevailed

the day the nation went to war, countrymen fighting against each other. Many of the men actually seemed to be excited, feeling as though this was just a lark. They talked as if the war would end quickly, with all the country's problems solved. How very wrong they were.

Elizabeth remembered the day Zachary came home saying he had joined the navy. He tried to console her, telling her he was going to be assigned to a unit that would remain in Richmond and would work as a strategist mapping out the defense tactics. But her tears would not cease. There she was with two babies. Morgan was only three and a half and Savannah just a year and a half. What would she do? How could she manage without Zachary?

What she feared would happen did happen. The war dragged on and on. Zachary was gone, as were most all of the men, young and old alike. Even her beloved Grandfather Morgan had joined the navy. He and Zachary, with their shipping experience, were vital to the defense of the surrounding waterways.

Letters between Zachary and Elizabeth were few and far between. He wrote her in April of 1862 that he and her Grandfather Morgan were assigned to the big ironclad Merrimack based at Norfolk. She recorded his letter in her journal:

My dearest Elizabeth,

It has been far too long since I've seen your face and held you in my arms. I long for the time to do just that. Don't let the children forget me. My heart belongs to the three of you. You are ever in my thoughts and prayers.

John and I have been assigned to the big ironclad, Merrimack, based at Norfolk. They say the flag officer is very knowledgeable so we are in good hands.

Pray along with me that this brutal war will soon be over and families can once again be reunited.

Answer as quickly as possible so I'll know how you are. It'll reach me sooner or later.

To Each His Own . . . your Zachary

The last of May, word reached Elizabeth that the Merrimack had been run aground near the mouth of the Elizabeth River. The flag officer removed his crew and then set her on fire. He did it to save them from imminent destruction.

Elizabeth was relieved to know that Zachary and her grandfather were saved from harm; however, she did not know where they were sent to from there. Communications from the military could be weeks, even months in coming. She never even knew if her letters would reach Zachary. But she wrote to him faithfully.

Elizabeth read from her journal:

. . . May 17, 1862: *Part of this ugly war has come to our beloved Willow Place.*

Seven tired and dirty Union soldiers stormed up on the porch, pounding on the front door. Molly Thatcher answered their rude knocking.

As they pushed their way into the foyer, I approached them from the parlor. Morgan was holding my hand and I was carrying Savannah.

It was evident the man in front of the group was an officer of the Union army. Upon seeing me, he turned white in the face and took two steps backward. For a moment he was speechless. He regained his composure quickly.

"Are you the mistress of the house?" he asked almost gently.

I nodded my head yes.

"I'm Lieutenant Jordan Bristol. These are my men. We seem to have gotten separated from our unit. We need food and water and then we will be on our way."

Two men standing on either side of this imposing stranger had their hands on their guns as if ready for any surprises.

I directed Molly to get them some food from the kitchen and told them there was a well in the backyard where they could get water.

The two men with their guns on ready began to say fresh and ugly things to me. Another of the men stepped forward and touched my hair.

Immediately Lt. Bristol barked out an order, "Leave the lady alone. We have no time to waste."

Molly returned with a flour sack of meat, bread and apples. Lt. Bristol took the sack and ordered the men to step outside.

He turned to Elizabeth and said, "You have no idea how much like my wife you look. The resemblance is uncanny. I also have two children at home. I can only imagine how frightened my wife would be under the same circumstances. I'm sorry for the intrusion. We will be on our way now. This is a savage war. It will do far more damage than good for all of us." With that said, he disappeared through the door . . .

After the war ended, Elizabeth told Zachary about the incident. He surprised her by saying he was the one who caught Lt. Bristol and his men and took them prisoner when they returned to join their unit. After the Merrimack had been intentionally grounded and set on fire, the crewmen from the ship were manning the guns on the bluff overlooking that part of the James River. They battled the Union warship Galena for over three hours. The ship had suffered countless hits and was badly damaged. When she began to take on water, they had to slip the Galena's cables and get back out of range. This was when Lt. Bristol and his men were trying to swim to the ship in order to escape with her. But Zachary and a few good men apprehended them short of their goal and took them prisoner.

Chapter 5

Godness . . . it was 9:30 and she had wiled away an hour and a half reading and reminiscing about times gone by! But Elizabeth couldn't seem to shake this feeling of nostalgia. She got up and walked to the window looking out over the breathtaking view of her beloved Willow Place. The lake was very calm adorned with the ever-present ducks taking their cruise around the lake. The dogwood trees were in full bloom, adding a backdrop of color to the green willow branches bowing so majestically to the beauty that surrounded them. Swimming into view were the two white swans that Zachary had bought for her when they were just babies. They were perfectly contented to stay on the lake and were favorites of the whole family.

Walking back to the desk, she selected one last journal from the shelf. Again she sat down in her grandfather's chair and turned to the entry dated April 9, 1865 and began to read:

. . . General Robert E. Lee surrendered the Confederate Army of Northern Virginia to Lieutenant General Ulysses S.

Grant. After four long and bitter years the war is finally over. But we have suffered great losses. It was decided that the people of Richmond should evacuate our beloved city, and even worse, that it be set on fire so as not to leave any gain for the Union Army. This meant that Morgan Carriage Company would be destroyed along with the rest of the businesses. This is such an emotional and radical change for all of us . . .

She closed the journal and placed it back on the shelf. The war years were filled with heartbreaks. Everyone's lives changed drastically. Where there had been safety and contentment, peril and anxiety prevailed. The men and boys were all gone, leaving the women and girls to keep the households going. Sickness and disease ran rampant, both at home and on the battlefields.

Wives and children died and were buried without the knowledge of their husbands and fathers who were fighting Lord knows where. The same held true for wives who were made widows and children made orphans, believing that their loved one would someday return to them safely.

Elizabeth, the children, her grandmother, and those who worked for them joined with others who fled Richmond before the city was intentionally burned. A camp was set up where they all survived as best they could.

Elizabeth remembered reading many months after the war that around 630,000 people lost their lives in this barbaric war and over one million were injured. To Elizabeth, one of the saddest things was brothers were sometimes fighting against brothers. Her prayer was that this would never happen again.

When Elizabeth and Zachary were finally reunited at the end of the war, she found that he had been shot through the left shoulder just weeks before the final day of surrender. After he was treated Zachary insisted on continuing with his work in the navy. Her beloved grandfather had looked after the wound daily so it never became infected. The wound healed nicely.

In returning to Willow Place from the makeshift camp, Elizabeth was surprised to see the house was still standing. A fire had been set to the backside of the house, but it went out before much damage was done. The house had evidently been used by some Union troops passing hastily through. They didn't wait around to see that the fire went out before it did major damage. Her grandparents' house on the other side of the lake was not in the path of the Union Army and was left standing. Elizabeth breathed a prayer of thanksgiving that things were not worse. She reasoned in her tired mind that God himself felt about Willow Place as she did and had protected it.

Four years had passed since the ending of the war. Things had been hard for everyone. The casualty list for Richmond had been a long one. But people had banded together and worked to clean up the ravages of war. People had helped people. The Golden Rule certainly prevailed. It seemed that hearts and minds had been turned toward God. There had been an influx of people to the First Wesleyan Church. A warmth and fellowship prevailed there that exceeded their expectations. This was good.

Chapter 6

AUGUST 16, 1880

Zachary and Elizabeth had just sat down at the large oak table in the kitchen for breakfast. He looked at Elizabeth and said, "You tossed and turned quite a bit last night. Didn't you rest well?"

"No I really didn't. I had Morgan on my mind. I've missed him a lot lately. I had hoped he would come back to Richmond to work after finishing school at William and Mary in May. Didn't you also think he would return to Richmond?"

"Yes, I really did, but there's still time. It's all right for him to have some leisure time to spend at the beach house in Williamsburg, and with mother and father in Norfolk. Of course, he's had some good sailing experiences with his Uncle Ben. He'll be fine."

Savannah bounced into the room with her usual cheerfulness. She went straight to her father and gave him a quick hug. Giving her mother a peck on the cheek, she started toward the stove to see what breakfast goodies were in the warmer. About that time Rosie appeared through the pantry door with a new jar of apple butter, Savannah's favorite.

"Sit down, my child, and let Rosie fix your breakfast plate," Rosie said with a mother hen's clucking ways.

Savannah had Rosie in her corner no matter what. They had bonded from the very beginning when Rosie came to work for them. Even though Savannah was 21 years old, Rosie still treated her like a child. Rosie Gilbert had come to work for the Bainbridge family when Molly Thatcher had to retire.

"What are your plans for today, Savannah?" her mother asked with a look of pride in her eyes.

"I'll be visiting little Merry Kelley as well as Jess Evans. Merry is as smart as a cricket. She's very attentive and asks questions if she isn't sure of something. She's a real pleasure to teach. Merry is going to be well enough to go back to school soon. I'll miss her."

"What about Jess? Is he a good student?" her father inquired.

"Knowing Jess Evans, what do you think? He's a little stinker. I'll be in the middle of a history lesson and he'll inquire, 'why does a snake shed its skin, Miss Savannah? Before I broke my leg I found a really big snakeskin! Here, let me show you just how big.' Then he begins stretching his arms as far as he can, exaggerating of course. But he's so cunning you can't help but be charmed by him, especially when he looks at you with those big brown, inquiring eyes."

Everyone who knew Savannah called her "the circuit rider." She got that nickname because she visited the homes of children that had to temporarily miss school, and tried to help them keep from getting behind in their schoolwork. It was totally a volunteer effort. She was very compassionate and loved to work with children. She also loved to ride as much as

Elizabeth, and could find her way into all the back roads and hill country of their community. Sometimes she rode as far as ten miles to help a child who needed some tutoring at home.

While Savannah finished breakfast, her mother and father excused themselves and walked to the front of the house and onto the porch. Zachary kissed Elizabeth goodbye and went down the steps to the carriage where George was waiting to take him to the rebuilt Morgan Carriage Company.

Elizabeth sat in one of the padded wrought iron chairs on the front porch and breathed in the fragrance of the many flowers and shrubs. The beauty of her surroundings overwhelmed her. When she reflected on how close they came to losing their home at Willow Place during the awful war, it made her even more grateful for this place. She shuddered at the thought that it might have burned to the ground.

Her beloved Grandmother Catherine had died at the age of 76 and her Grandfather John at 78. They had been in good health all those years until the last year of their lives. They had enjoyed their two great grandchildren, Morgan and Savannah. Those were cherished years for the children. Their lives were made richer by the love and care given to them during their formative years by these two very special people.

The whole family owed John and Catherine Morgan so much. During the years that John owned Morgan Shipping Company in Williamsburg he had been a wise investor. He had bought land in prime locations, invested in stocks and was very shrewd in buying gold bars and gold coins for years. He had talked with Zachary in 1857, the year that Morgan was born, advising that they should put more of their investment into the purchase of gold. These were uncertain times politically. John felt investing in gold would be a way to protect the family's worth. Because of his wisdom they had not lost everything due to the war. Yes, they did lose their stocks, and the paper money became worthless. But their gold investments were in a protective place. It gave them a base on which to rebuild after the war. The value of his land investments only increased.

It took several years to rebuild the carriage company. The last six years had been good ones. They had made great strides in the designs and comfort of their carriages. Zachary had enlarged the plant and hired more workers.

Elizabeth rose to her feet and said out loud, "Enough of this wool gathering! I must get busy." She went inside and called out to Savannah as she started down the hall to the kitchen.

"I'm still in the kitchen, Mother."

"What time are you leaving to go to the Kelley's?"

"I'll leave about 10:00 o'clock. Why do you ask? Is there something I can do for you?"

"Yes. I'm going to write a letter to Morgan. Will you please take it to the post office and mail it on your way to the Kelley's?"

"I'll be happy to. As a matter of fact, I'll also write him a note. I miss him terribly. I thought he would be back home by now."

Chapter 7

August 25, 1880
WILLIAMSBURG

*M*organ finished off the last of the goulash, washing it down with a cold glass of milk. He had gotten pretty good at improvising with leftovers. He reckoned he just might be able to win a prize with this dish!

After cleaning up his mess he sat down on the sun porch and rifled through his mail. He had hit the jackpot. There was a letter from his mother and his sister, Savannah. He couldn't help but notice his mother's beautiful penmanship as he read his name on the envelope . . . Mr. Morgan Bainbridge. He quickly opened it and began to read.

AUGUST 16, 1880
RICHMOND, VIRGINIA

Dearest Morgan,

Your father and I were speaking of you just this morning. We miss you very much. We had hoped you might come home to Richmond to work since you've finished your education. *What plans do you have for the future, or do you know yet? Let us* hear from you soon.

Morgan, I want to tell you how proud we are of you. You've been an honorable son. The joy you've brought us has caused our hearts to sing. No wonder David wrote in the Psalms, "Lo, children are an heritage of the Lord:" Your father and I have taken this responsibility very seriously. We never want to fail you and Savannah.

How are Greg and Mary Ann Maxwell? We hope you see Phillip and Jane often. Give them our warm regards. Savannah is still our "circuit rider" and loves every minute of it. She's so good with the children. She's our delight.

> Your father sends his love.
> Affectionately,
> Mother

Morgan, still holding his mother's letter, looked out over the James River and watched the sailboats that were passing by. A feeling of nostalgia swept over him. He knew he was a fortunate young man to have the love and respect of his parents. Would that everyone could have been raised in such a loving home. He felt safe just thinking about it. But he knew it was time he went back to Richmond and told his parents his plans . . . plans he knew they would not really want to hear.

He smiled as he read Savannah's letter. She facetiously told him that she had to do back breaking work since he'd been gone to college. She said she needed him to come home and rescue her. It was her way of telling her big brother that she missed him.

A feeling of homesickness gripped him. It had been great going to William and Mary College in Williamsburg. Living at the beach house had been perfect. What a good investment this place had been. His Great Grandfather Morgan was always a visionary. He had put aside gold coins to assure his great grandson's education and to provide a good nest egg for his namesake's future. As a result, Morgan could pursue his dream, a dream he would have to share with his parents.

Morgan and Greg Maxwell, his best friend, spent the next day sailing. In the late afternoon they brought the boat in to dock and 'charted' their personal course for the near future. Greg would tell his parents of their plans while Morgan went to Richmond to break the news to Elizabeth and Zachary. This was a venture the boys felt they had to pursue.

Chapter 8

September 3, 1880
Richmond

Savannah came running to him as he stepped down from the train, "Morgan, Morgan, you're here, finally! Oh, it's so good to see my brother," she exclaimed as she ran into his big strong arms.

Giving her a warm hug, he held her at arms length and said, "Let me look at you, little sister. You don't look as if you've done any back breaking work lately!"

"Looks can be deceiving. Where are your bags? Is that the only one you brought?"

"This is it. Where's the carriage? Did George drive you in?" Morgan inquired.

"No, I wanted to come for you alone, so I came in the buggy and parked down at the livery stable. Let's go get some lemonade at the Sandwich Shop before heading for home."

As they sipped the cold lemonade Savannah asked, "What have you been doing this summer since you graduated from William and Mary? I notice you're sporting a nice tan."

"As you might expect I've been doing a lot of sailing. Uncle Ben and I spent a good deal of time together. Aunt Andrea is as much of a 'beach bum' as Uncle Ben. They've really treated me right. I've also spent time with Grandfather and Grandmother Bainbridge, Uncle Tom and Aunt Joyce. What's been going on in your life?"

"I thought you'd never ask! Do you remember Vann Baker? He's known in these parts as being one of the best horsemen around. He and his family breed and raise horses. Remember, they bought that big spread about five miles south of Willow Place and built a sprawling house."

"Are you trying to make a point, Savannah, or do I need to play a guessing game?"

"Well, do you remember him?"

"I seem to have a slight recollection of him. Is he that squatty, bow-legged, crooked-nosed fellow?" Morgan feigned innocence in his question.

"Morgan Bainbridge, you're impossible! You're just jealous of his good looks."

"You've really got me guessing, little sister. What about this Vann Baker?"

"Well, I've been seeing him. And I like him very much."

"Do mother and father know about him?"

"Of course they do. I had to get permission to go out with him. They are impressed with his manners. But they don't know just how much I like him. Neither does Vann," Savannah confided.

"Well, do you think I should check him out for you . . . just ask around to see what people in the area think of him, maybe?

I know several fellahs who just might know," Morgan said reflectively.

"You can do that, but please don't tell them why you're asking."

"Never fear, little sister, I'll be very discreet."

"We best be on our way now. Mother and father will be sitting on the porch, looking up the road for their prodigal son to return. We've all missed you terribly, Morgan."

Sure enough, when they reached Willow Place their mother and father were waiting on the front porch. They both ran down the steps to greet Morgan as soon as he stepped out of the buggy. Morgan gave his father a bear hug, patting him on the back several times. Then he lifted his mother up and swung her around a couple of times. They all laughed joyously at their son's homecoming. He had come home for Easter, but that was almost five months ago.

Tuesday, September 4th, was a stormy day. The lightening flashed and the thunder rolled most all day. The rains were torrential at times. It didn't make it any easier for Morgan to tell his family about his plans. The inclement weather made the message seem worse. But finally he knew the time had come. They were seated in the parlor after supper with a fire in the fireplace to take the autumn-like chill out of the air.

"I've really come home to discuss my future plans with all of you. I plan to go north to parts unknown to me, perhaps New York, Philadelphia or even Chicago. I want to see what I can do on my own and discover what's out there. With a degree in business I know I'm well equipped to take on this venture. Just how long I'll be gone I don't know, but I know that I'm going."

Morgan had looked from one face to the other as he spoke. His father looked surprised, but serious and reflective. Savannah gasped in surprise. He had to turn away from the look of sadness on his mother's kind and beautiful face.

"I know this is unexpected and difficult for all of you to understand. The wounds of war have not really healed, Father. The South still feels betrayed and bitter toward the North. You might view me as a traitor to my heritage. But this is a big country and there are many opportunities out there. All of you know I have an adventurous spirit. I must see things for myself. Besides, I almost feel compelled to go, and New York will most likely be my destination."

"When do you plan to leave, son?" his father inquired.

"First, I'll tell you that Greg Maxwell is also going. He and I have discussed this idea for the past year, just between us. He is telling his parents this very evening. We will be leaving on Monday, September 24th. I'll be staying here for Savannah's birthday on the 19th before returning to Williamsburg," Morgan replied.

Elizabeth had not moved since Morgan made his announcement. Morgan crossed the room and sat down beside her. Taking her hand between his he said, "Mother, I know this is hard on you. I know what you're thinking. You're reflecting on what your father, my grandfather, John Lee Morgan, whom neither of us ever knew, did. But that happened 40-plus years ago. Since we are a sharing family, Savannah and I know the story of the past. But remember how the shadow of the past almost ruined yours and father's chance of being married? Do you, mother? Please, look at me. I'm your son. This is 1880. The Industrial Revolution has spread to the United States. We've become the worlds fore most industrialized nation fueled by abundant resources and technological advances. I want to be a part of this. I very much want your blessings in this venture. Mother, please!"

Chapter 8

Elizabeth was very pale. In spite of the logic of Morgan's argument, the past swept over her like a flood. She remembered the conversation she had with her beloved Grandmother Catherine about when her only child, John Lee, left home to try it on his own. He was just 24 years old and they never saw him again. Of course, John Lee Morgan, her father, had married Victoria, her mother, and she was conceived. But he died, accidentally, before she was born. Now *her son*, Morgan, who is also 24, wants to leave home and try it on his own! How on earth could she give Morgan her blessings? The scripture from Proverbs filled her heart as though sent directly from the Lord at that moment. "Trust in the Lord with all thine heart; and lean not unto thine own understanding. In all thy ways acknowledge him, and he shall direct thy paths." Just last week she had read in Genesis a scripture that had really impressed her . . . "The Lord watch between me and thee, when we are absent one from another." Then she had turned to Psalm 91 and read, "For he shall give his angels charge over thee, to keep thee in all thy ways. They shall bear thee up in *their* hands, lest thou dash thy foot against a stone."

"Mother?" Morgan said again, gently.

"Son, I can't say I'm overjoyed at your announcement. It's come as a great surprise to me . . . to us. We had expectations that you would come back to Richmond and join your father at the carriage company. He could use your help, you know. But if this is what you want for your life, we must accept it and certainly give you our blessings."

"I'll not disappoint you. And I'll stay in touch. I'm not saying that I'll stay up north. But I want to look around and see what they have going. I also might tell you that Mary Ann and I have been seeing each other on a regular basis lately. I'm very much interested in her. I believe the feeling is mutual.

She is another reason for staying in touch with my 'home-land,'" Morgan said.

Elizabeth was awake into the wee hours of the morning. She had a lot of thinking as well as a lot of praying to do. Finally she became willing to lay Morgan on the altar, putting him completely in the Lord's hands. A feeling of complete peace swept over her and blessed sleep came, finally.

Chapter 9

SEPTEMBER 6, THURSDAY

*S*avannah cancelled all her appointments to spend as much time as possible with Morgan. They talked and talked, confiding in one another about their deep feelings for Vann and Mary Ann. They enjoyed horseback riding, went fishing, and hiked in the back acres of Willow Place where they used to go as teenagers. The two of them visited some of Morgan's old friends. He made some inquiries about Vann Baker. All the reports he got were good ones. This was a relief to Savannah.

On Thursday Morgan promised to take his mother shopping. Savannah needed to go to the Miller's home to do some extra work with little Adam Miller. They lived further away than any child she had gone to tutor. But Mr. Cochran said Adam had already missed seven days of school because of the red measles and needed some help. She planned to be home by the time her mother and Morgan returned from their shopping trip.

Rosie had packed Savannah a good lunch. She decided to ride Bonnie because her horse, Thunder, had a sore right front leg and she didn't want to stress it further. Bonnie was easy to be spooked but was a fun horse to ride. After saddling up and filling her saddlebag with school supplies for Adam, she called Shaggy, her constant companion on these trips, and headed south. She had never visited the Miller's home before but had been given good directions. Riding south past the Baker's horse farm, which was several miles out, she turned north on Rock Hill Road. By this time she knew Shaggy was getting tired, so she stopped at the creek to let him get some water. She ate a chicken leg for lunch and gave one to Shaggy. She stretched out on her back and Shaggy lay down beside her. After a short rest she patted her faithful dog's head and said, "Come on Shaggy dog, we've got to go now."

The rest of the trip was rugged. The narrow road was rutted pretty badly so she held Shaggy in her arms as she rode. She carefully reined Bonnie until she reached the Miller's home.

Mrs. Miller was glad to see her. They didn't get many visitors up here in the hill country. They exchanged pleasantries and had some fresh baked bread spread with butter and honey along with a cup of cinnamon tea.

Kate Miller was a pretty lady in a plain way. She was wearing a faded cotton dress made from flour sack material with blue flowers. Her apron was made of a solid blue fabric. Her clothing was spotlessly clean as well as her house. She had her hair pulled back and tied with a faded blue ribbon. She looked admiringly as she touched the cuff of Savannah's long-sleeved blouse that was trimmed with embroidery.

"Miss Savannah, that's a right pretty outfit you're wearing. Your blouse matches your riding skirt perfectly. I've always admired stylish clothes," Kate said.

"Why, thank you, Kate. How kind of you to notice. And I thank you for the refreshments you've served. The hot bread is especially delicious."

Savannah noticed that she and Kate were almost exactly the same size. Perhaps she could share some of her things with Kate. She made a mental note to do just that.

Adam still had a rash from the measles. Savannah remembered when she had them, how much they itched and how she thought they would never go away. She assured Adam they would. He had not had a very bad case of the measles, but still had to be quarantined to protect others from catching them. Normally measles affected the eyes, but Adam's had given him little trouble. It was obvious he had been well cared for.

Savannah helped Adam get caught up on his schoolwork, as much as she felt he could do under the circumstances. She then read him a couple of stories from a book she had brought. Adam dropped off to sleep just as she finished the last story.

Savannah left the Miller's house about 2:15 in the afternoon. The wind began to blow and she saw a dark, ominous cloud rising just ahead of her. She didn't like the looks of it. Shaggy began to bark which he seldom ever did. Suddenly there was a sharp, jagged streak of lightening and a loud clap of thunder that seemed to rumble on forever. She had been riding about ten minutes. Elizabeth decided to take a short cut through the woods, thinking it would come out at Snake Creek and put her much closer to home than the long way. The terrain was much rougher than she anticipated which slowed her down. The wind blew against her face and the torrential rain beat against her body. She worried about Shaggy. She knew he was scared as well as Bonnie. About that time Bonnie lost her footing, stumbled and threw Savannah headlong into a deep ravine.

When she came to herself, she realized she was lying on her left side in water from the waist down. Shaggy was standing near her face whimpering. She tried to get up but couldn't move. Pain shot through her like hot liquid. She was fading in and out of consciousness. The rain was still coming down steadily. Savannah knew she was going to have to get out of the water. She prayed and asked the Lord to help her. She could still move her arms, so she tugged and pulled herself onto drier ground. But the effort drained her of her strength. The rain had stopped finally. The blood she tasted in her mouth was coming from a deep gash over her left eye. It was trickling down her face.

"Shaggy, go find Bonnie. Go boy. Go find her."

But Shaggy didn't budge. He laid his head on his front paws and stared at Savannah with a mournful look.

Savannah always felt she was tough and prided herself in being strong. Taking care of Thunder, her red roan quarter horse, gave her great satisfaction. She kept his coat washed and brushed, cleaned his hooves and even cleaned his stall quite often. Saddling him up took strength. She knew she was going to have to use that same kind of strength to get out of this mess. One thing for sure, she had to get her boot off her left foot. If not, the swelling would cut off the circulation completely. Finally, she managed to get it off. This relieved some of the pressure that was causing her so much pain in her leg and foot. But the pain in her left hip was piercing. It was beginning to get dark. Shaggy lay even closer to Savannah. Much of the night was spent in so much pain she would forget where she was.

Morning finally came and Savannah knew she had to get to the top of the ravine. She began the torturous climb. Actually, she dug her hands into the dirt and drug herself inch by painful inch. Thank goodness she had worn a thick, long-sleeved blouse. But her hands were torn and bleeding from the grueling ordeal.

Her clothes were still damp from yesterday's heavy rain and the plunge into the soggy ravine, causing some uncomfortable chaffing. She was so thirsty. Her head was throbbing from the deep gash, but at least it had stopped bleeding. Half way up the climb she felt she would never make it.

In a very weak voice she pleaded, "Shaggy dog, please go get help. Go boy. Go get help."

Shaggy would run a distance, barking as he went. Then he would come back and lick her face. It was evident he wasn't going to leave her.

By the time she got to the top of the hill it was nightfall once again. She was so thirsty and felt very hot. She began to hallucinate. She felt there were bugs all over her. In her fevered delirium, she imagined she saw Bonnie coming near her only to turn and run away just as he would get close enough for Savannah to get hold of the reins. She could faintly hear Shaggy barking furiously before she slipped into a deep vacuum of unconsciousness.

Chapter 10

SEPTEMBER 6ᵀᴴ
WILLOW PLACE

*M*organ and Elizabeth had gotten home from shopping and were having coffee in the library. They expected Savannah to come bouncing in at any minute.

"Mother, how did Savannah get involved in home tutoring?" Morgan asked as he looked out the library window watching the swans on the lake.

"Mr. Cochran, of the West Richmond School, approached her about helping out. He had two very bright students from the same family who had to be out of school due to a family crisis. If Savannah had not tutored them, they would have failed the whole year because they had to miss six weeks of school. Savannah found it to be very rewarding and has been doing it for the last two years. She's very happy working with the children."

"Savannah is a remarkable young lady. She has looks, smarts and is a loving, caring person. I'm fortunate that she is my little sister, wouldn't you agree?" Morgan asked with pride.

Five o'clock came and went and Savannah wasn't home yet. Morgan walked out back of the house and headed toward the barn to see if she had ridden in without his seeing her. Albert Taylor, the overseer of Willow Place, was striding toward Morgan leading Bonnie who was still fully saddled.

"Why are you bringing Bonnie to the house, Albert? Where is Savannah?"

"I don't know where Miss Savannah is. Bonnie came galloping up to the barn and whinnied, almost frightened me to death. I grabbed her reins and came immediately to tell you that she came in alone. Miss Savannah is nowhere to be found."

"Here, let me look in the saddlebag. Savannah's water canteen is almost full. Most of her lunch is uneaten. None of Bonnie's gear is broken. The saddle is still secure. Bonnie isn't lathered indicating she's been running. Perhaps Savannah stopped near here to rest and failed to tie Bonnie up and Bonnie just wandered off leaving her behind. Did Shaggy go with Savannah when she left?"

"Yes sir, he did. After Miss Savannah saddled Bonnie up, before she left, she told me she would be home by three or three-thirty at the latest," Albert said with a troubled look.

Morgan heard his father's carriage driving up. "Stay right here, Albert. I'll be right back," Morgan said as he ran around the side of the house.

His Father was stepping down out of the carriage when Morgan reached him. "Come with me Father, hurry!"

Surprised at this greeting, Zachary followed Morgan at a fast pace. When he saw Bonnie and Albert standing in the back yard he wondered what was going on.

Elizabeth was looking out the library window when Zachary's carriage drove up. She saw Morgan running toward Zachary and then both of them sprinted out of sight. Elizabeth walked hurriedly through the kitchen and out the back door where she joined them.

"What is it, son? Is something wrong with Bonnie? She looks fine to me," Zachary commented.

"Savannah left this morning, Father, going to the Luke Miller house up in the hill country to tutor Luke's boy. Bonnie has just come into the barn alone. Neither Savannah nor Shaggy was with her. Something's not right here."

Elizabeth looked first at her husband and then at her son, "You must look for Savannah. It'll be dark in about an hour and a half. Time is of the essence!"

"Albert, get a couple of the men, saddle up the horses. Let's take at least three lanterns. Go quickly. We'll meet you at the stables," Zachary directed.

He turned to Morgan, "Get some canteens filled with fresh water. Elizabeth, have Rosie pack some food. Hurry! We don't know what has happened but we need to be prepared. And, Elizabeth, get a soft blanket and give it to Morgan."

The five of them rode out heading south. When they came to the Baker's horse farm, Morgan slowed down. Vann was sitting on the front steps of their sprawling home.

"What's up?" he yelled out to Morgan as they were passing.

"Savannah's missing. Want to join us?"

"I'll catch up to you!" Vann yelled as he ran toward his stables.

Vann caught up with them and asked for details. Morgan explained. They rode noticing everything as they went but found nothing unusually disturbed. Turning north as they reached Rock Hill Road, they discovered deep gullies washed in the narrow roadbed. They had made good time until now, even though the rain had pelted them all the way. Finally the Miller house came into view. Morgan leaped from his horse and bounded up the porch steps. Knocking urgently on the front door, it opened immediately.

"Good evening, Luke. Savannah wouldn't still be here, would she?"

"No. She was gone when I got home."

He looked back into the room and asked, "Kate, what time did Miss Savannah leave this afternoon?"

Kate came to the door and answered, "She left at 2:15. She said she wanted to be home by 3:15. Why, is something wrong?"

"I'm afraid so, Mrs. Miller. Her horse, Bonnie, came home without Savannah. We must go immediately and search for her. Darkness will be settling in fast," Morgan said, tipping his hat.

"Hold on and I'll saddle up and go with you. I know these parts pretty good," Luke said.

The rain was letting up somewhat. They searched down trails here and there until it was so dark the lanterns were not much help. The terrain was so uneven and rough they decided to make camp until daylight.

Zachary walked away from the campfire by himself. He raised his eyes heavenward.

"Lord, this is my child that is lost somewhere in these woods that surround us. But, she is not lost to you, Lord. You know exactly where she is. Please lead us to her. Protect her until we can get to her. She must be so frightened and might even be injured. I have to place her in Your hands. I know from experience that Your hands are the safest place she could be. Help us find her soon. Amen."

Daylight finally came. They separated into two groups. Luke, Zachary, Albert and Jim rode in one direction, Morgan, Vann and Bart in another. They would circle and then meet back in the road. This went on all day long. They called Savannah's name as well as Shaggy's. Nighttime came again with no success. Zachary and Morgan were really worried by now. They wanted to keep looking, even in the dark, but they knew the horses needed rest. It wouldn't do for one or more of them to step into a low place and break a leg. It just made more sense to wait until daylight to search more successfully.

Tomorrow would be September 8th, Saturday. By daylight Savannah would have been missing 40 hours. They simply had to find her! Zachary asked all the men to make a circle around the campfire.

"I want to ask all of you to pray with me that we'll find Savannah in the morning. There's no doubt that she's injured. She's been without food and water for at least 40 hours. We've done all we know to do. We must have the Lord's help and I have to believe that He will lead us to her. Please bow your heads. 'Lord, you well remember when Ben and I were in that scary storm at sea in the sailboat. The storm was so violent we thought we wouldn't escape with our lives. During those two terrible days we humbly sought your help. Elizabeth was praying for us as well as the rest of the family. You heard those prayers and answered them and delivered us from the storm. Now, Lord, Savannah is in a storm of her own. She needs You to deliver her. All of us here are depending on You to do just that. Thank you, Lord, for this blessing. Amen.' Let's try to exercise faith, gentlemen," Zachary said, almost in a whisper.

Chapter 11

SEPTEMBER 8TH, SATURDAY
WILLOW PLACE

Elizabeth and her friends were all in the parlor. Pastor David Autry, his wife, Emily, and several of the First Wesleyan members had come to Willow Place to wait for word about Savannah. It was 10:00 A.M. Elizabeth's mind was so tired. She had tried to think the best. But so much time had passed that she began to fear the worst. Her mind went back to the time Zachary and Ben were in the terrible storm in the cruiser sailboat on Chesapeake Bay. She remembered how the Lord had come to their rescue because of prayer. She appreciated Pastor Autry and close friends from the church coming to offer their prayerful support. She could not help but think of the scripture, "Bear ye one another's burdens."

Rosie came into the parlor with a tray of hot coffee and some warm muffins. Her eyes were red and swollen from crying. Elizabeth noticed how frail she looked. She had scarcely slept since Thursday.

Emily, an accomplished pianist, sat down at Savannah's piano and began to play the beautiful old hymn, "Amazing Grace." Elizabeth listened to the message of the words as they played over in her mind. It had never sounded so sweet or given her more comfort. She could not help but wonder if Savannah would ever play the piano again. She had taken after her Grandmother Bainbridge and was quite a talented pianist. "Please, Lord, send Savannah home to us," Elizabeth prayed.

. . . THAT SAME MORNING . . .

Luke Miller said, "Look, fellahs, we've searched all the way to the bottom of where Snake Creek flows near Willow Road and we've found nothing. Suppose in the rain Savannah got mixed up and turned right off of Rock Hill Road thinking she was taking the trail that led to Snake Creek. We have concentrated on the left side. Let's go back to the top and comb the right side more carefully."

Zachary answered, "You lead the way, Luke."

The weary and haggard men took on new courage at this suggestion, pushing their tired animals just a little harder.

. . . AT THE TOP OF THE RAVINE . . .

Shaggy ran round and round Savannah as she lay motionless. He licked her face but she did not move. He seemed to sense what he must do. Taking one last look at Savannah, he began barking and running back from the way they had come.

He ran for several miles, stopped suddenly, and perked up his ears. Then he began to bark furiously.

"Listen! Listen!" Zachary exclaimed, "That's Shaggy. That's Shaggy barking. I'm sure of it! Here Shaggy, here Shaggy. Come here boy!" Zachary said as he began to ride toward the sound of the barking.

They were already deep into the woods when Shaggy appeared in front of them. Morgan dismounted quickly taking Shaggy into his arms, giving him a big hug. He was muddy and really looked the part of a shaggy dog. His paws were bleeding from the rough terrain he had traveled. But they had to put him down and let him lead them to Savannah. They could not believe how far he had come looking for help. Shaggy ran straight to Savannah and began licking her face. Zachary literally leapt from his horse and got to her first. Morgan was close behind him. Tears ran down both their faces as they saw Savannah lying so still and lifeless. They noticed the deep wound over her left eye. Her left ankle was swollen to twice its size. Her hands were raw and had dried blood caked on them.

Vann reacted quickly. He got his canteen and wet his bandana, placing it gently on her forehead. Then he attempted to get her to drink some water. She was able to taste it as it spilled into her partially opened mouth. She aroused somewhat and opened her eyes, but only to reveal a blank stare. Vann persisted in getting her to sip some water. She was burning up with fever.

Luke found a couple of sticks. Vann took off his outer shirt and began tearing it into strips. Using the strips and sticks they were able to fashion a splint to stabilize her ankle. But the procedure was so painful it penetrated Elizabeth's unconsciousness and caused her to moan pitifully.

Albert, Jim and Bart appeared with several willowy tree limbs. They tied them together with strong cord that Bart had in his saddlebag. They then covered the branches with a blanket to form a makeshift stretcher. Placing Savannah carefully upon it, they took turns carrying her. They kept wet bandanas on her face trying to keep her cool.

It was a long, slow process to get Savannah back to Rock Hill Road. They had sent Jim to Vann's place to bring back a wagon. Jim had put a lot of blankets in the wagon to make Savannah as comfortable as possible.

It had been a long ordeal but they finally got Savannah to East Richmond Hospital and under the care of their doctor and close family friend, Dr. David Blake. He was the surgeon general of East Richmond. His wife, Kim, was supervisor of nursing. They had worked here for more than twenty years. The hospital had almost doubled in size during their tenure. Elizabeth had been doing volunteer work here for just as many years. As she sat by Savannah's bedside she felt right at home.

Dr. Blake and Kim had been with Savannah since she arrived yesterday afternoon about one o'clock. Elizabeth and Zachary watched as they attended Savannah all through the night. They had packed her in ice to cool her fever. The wound on her head had been cleaned thoroughly and sutured. Dr. Blake didn't think her ankle was broken. He called it a painful sprain. They discovered a puncture wound on her left hip that had become infected. It was cleaned and treated. Now it was just a wait and see process. Savannah still had not fully regained consciousness. She would mumble and open her eyes, but with no sign of recognizing anyone. Dr. Blake said the blow to her head had caused a concussion.

After they had done all that could be done for her, the four of them held hands in a circle and Dr. Blake prayed one of the sweetest prayers Elizabeth and Zachary had ever heard.

"Our kind and loving Heavenly Father, we have need of Thee at this hour. You tell us in your word, 'My grace is sufficient for thee: for my strength is made perfect in weakness.' We certainly admit to our weakness this day. In our human weakness we treated Savannah. We are looking for Your strength to do the rest. We are well aware that healing comes from You, our Creator. We stand on the promises of Your word. We have watched Savannah grow up from a baby. She's one of Your children. She was injured while doing good things for others. Please be mindful of this. We ask these things in the name of our Lord and Savior, Jesus Christ. Amen."

Morgan and Vann were in the waiting room hoping to hear some good news soon. Their conversation centered on Savannah and the condition in which they had found her. Her dog, Shaggy, was the hero. Rosie had treated his little paws, given him a good bath, fed him well and let him sleep on Savannah's bed.

"Morgan, I don't know if Savannah has told you that she and I have been seeing each other for the past six months. This has been with the blessings of your parents. I don't mind telling you that I've grown to care deeply for her. These last 48 hours have shown me just how much," Vann confessed.

"As a matter of fact, Vann, she did tell me that you were dating. She spoke well of you to me. She's my only sister. Her welfare is very important to me. I hope you'll keep this in mind," Zachary replied.

"You can count on it, Morgan. I don't know that Savannah feels the same as I do. But I intend to find out as soon as she is better."

Chapter 12

SEPTEMBER 19ᵀᴴ, WEDNESDAY

*I*t had been twelve days since they had found Savannah and brought her to the hospital. Due to excellent care and many prayers, she had rebounded. The two deep wounds she suffered had almost completely healed. Dr. Blake assured her the scar over her left eye would not be very noticeable in a few weeks. Her hands were still tender, but the deeper scrapes were almost well. Her badly sprained ankle would take longer to heal. She needed to keep her leg elevated as much as possible to help keep the swelling to a minimum. She still walked with a limp. Dr. Blake said it would take about six weeks for it to get back to normal.

Today was her 21st birthday. It was a glorious day to Savannah. She loved her birthday, every single minute of it. It might be a lot of other people's birthday, too, but it belonged only to her as far as she was concerned! It was her gift from God.

Knowing how Savannah had always felt about her birthday her mother, father and Morgan made it a special day each year for her. Today was no different.

Breakfast began the celebration. Rosie prepared French toast with hot maple syrup, crisp bacon and coffee. Then the family presented her their gifts.

She removed the soft tissue paper from around the gift her mother and father had given her. She gasped as she lifted it from the box. It was an oil painting of the two of them, a perfect likeness, in a gilt-edged frame. Tears of joy welled up in her eyes. What a perfect gift.

"After my accident," Savannah said, "I began to think about what a precious gift life is. I thought about how I came to be. It dawned on me, possibly for the first time, that because you two met, fell in love with each other and married, I was born. Your love and God's love created me. It was a very sobering thought. The thought also came to me that, rightfully, I should pay tribute to you, my parents, on my birthday. I want you both to know that I am awed when I think of all the things you have done for me through the years. The most important things have been spiritual. Your hands have turned thousands of pages in the Bible as you have searched the scriptures. Only our Heavenly Father knows the countless times your hands have been clasped in prayer for Morgan and me. Not only have you blessed us, but you have blessed others by the way you've lived. You both stood by me during my ordeal. I think it's time that I thank *you* and celebrate *you* on my birthday! So I salute *you both* this September 19th, 1880!"

Zachary and Elizabeth were speechless at this special daughter's declaration of love.

"Savannah, you know that I have always loved you, my little sister; but never more than today. I thank God that His hand of protection was upon you when we were not there to

64

protect you. I wouldn't have missed your 21st birthday for anything! Here is my gift to you," Morgan said as he handed her an oblong, slender package.

After removing the wrappings, Savannah exclaimed as she saw what was inside. It was one of the now popular, French created, folding carriage parasols. It was delicate and beautifully made with elaborate silk and black lace. This had become an object of high fashion. Many of the ladies were now carrying them.

"Morgan, you always come up with the nicest gifts. How can I ever thank you? But I do! I'm so glad you're here for my birthday. Thank you for the gift and the time you put into selecting it."

She gave each of them a warm hug of gratitude.

Savannah's Sunday school class was invited over for her birthday luncheon. It was served in the formal dining room. The table was overlaid with a linen and lace tablecloth. They used the still beautiful willow patterned dinnerware that belonged to Great Grandmother Savannah Baldwin. Rosie fixed a delicious meal. She had cooked a three-layered chocolate cake for Savannah's birthday. Rosie served hot cinnamon coffee with the cake. They all sat around the table and insisted that Savannah tell them about being lost in the woods, her injuries and her rescue.

Savannah rested after the luncheon was over. She had a date that evening with Vann Baker. She wanted to feel and look her very best.

Vann called for her at 7:00. She was wearing her dark blue taffeta dress that made her eyes look bluer than ever. The neck of the dress was round and buttoned down the back with small covered buttons that matched the ones on the long fitted sleeves. The crinolines she was wearing made the full skirt billow around her, and the perky bustle added just the right touch. Her blonde hair was down to her shoulders framing her face like a halo. She smiled her enchanting smile when Vann came into the library where she was waiting for him. Her smile accentuated her charming dimples. This is when she looked most like her mother.

Zachary and Elizabeth greeted Vann warmly. They would be forever grateful to him for helping them find Savannah, having the forethought to make quick decisions about getting her to the hospital, and then sitting with Morgan until the crisis was over.

Vann was very much the cowboy. His skin had been tanned by the sun and wind. His eyes were rich dark brown and his hair as black as midnight. He wasn't terribly tall, about five feet eleven inches. His sinewy build made folks take a second look. His countenance was somewhat moody, like that of Heathcliff of "Wuthering Heights," until he smiled. The first time Savannah saw his dazzling smile it took her breath away!

"Mr. and Mrs. Bainbridge, I have tickets to a Steven Foster stage production of 'Carry Me Back to Old Virginia.' It's being presented by a new musical group that's supposed to be very good. We might be a little late getting home. Will that be alright?"

"Just take care of Savannah and don't let her get too tired," Zachary said.

"She will be my first concern, I assure you," Vann replied.

The musical was very entertaining, but it wasn't as long as they had expected. By 8:45 they were back in the carriage and on their way to a uniquely romantic park.

The history of Zachary and Elizabeth's special place 'in a garden' in Williamsburg was not known to Vann as he took Savannah to the beautifully manicured garden outside the Museum of Arts building in downtown Richmond. It was known as the Joe Stock Memorial Park in Lafayette Square. Mr. Stock had been a great supporter of civic endeavors for Richmond. He was a local businessman and had the interest of the town and its people at heart. The focal point in the garden was a pond with water lilies. Wrought iron benches, donated by the town's ironworks factory owner, had been placed throughout the garden as well as around the pond. There were two other couples strolling in this picturesque setting. The full moon on this warm September evening gave a magical glow to their surroundings.

Vann chose a bench close to where the carriage had stopped so Savannah would not have far to walk.

Vann turned to Savannah and said, "These past six months that we've been seeing each other have become very important to me. I think about you day and night. When Morgan and the others rode by our place on September 6th and he yelled out to me that you were lost, a feeling of despair swept over me. When we finally found you, injured to the point of unconsciousness, I don't mind telling you I was scared to death of losing you. Immediately I began to take stock of my life. I fell shy of the mark. I knew I needed to pray for you but would my prayers be heard? I've been brought up in a loving Christian home, so prayer is no stranger to me. I can tell you that I fixed things up between me and the Lord. I'm well aware of how He answered all our prayers for your complete recovery. I've said all of this to let you know how very special you are to me."

Savannah sat quietly for a while. She could hardly believe this was happening on her birthday. She had fancied in her mind what it might be like to hear Vann say he cared for her. In reality, it was far greater than she ever imagined. *He said that I am very important to him and that he thinks about me day and night. Isn't this the same as saying that he loves me? And he says I'm special to him . . .*

"Are you alright, Savannah? Have I said something wrong?" Vann inquired, interrupting her thoughts.

"I've been trying to comprehend all that you've said to me, Vann. It pleases me very much that you say I'm special to you," Savannah replied.

"Dare I be so bold as to tell you that I not only think you're special but I'm deeply in love with you?" Vann urgently asked.

Normally, Savannah never thought of herself as being one bit shy. She usually spoke her mind if she was sure about something. But this thing called love was a different avenue to her. She knew that she loved Vann, with all her heart, but it was scary for her to admit it out loud. What if she told him and then he changed his mind about her? Should she trust her emotions and tell him that she loved him too, or should she wait awhile? She had hardly looked at him all this time.

Savannah scooted down the bench, turned sideways so she could look into his face . . . into his eyes. The moonlight was so bright it was almost like daylight. She searched his face, his 'Heathcliff' face, looked deep into those brown eyes and knew the answer right away. She reached up and traced his mouth with her fingertips, which brought on that breath-taking smile of his.

"Dare I tell you I think you're special and that I'm deeply in love with you, Vann Baker?"

That's when the cowboy came out in Vann. He leapt to his feet and let out a big 'yippee,' picked her up, swinging her around a couple of times before setting her down gently and kissing her passionately.

"You are my girl now. We have a lot of things to talk about, but I best get you back home if I expect to get to see you again with your parents' blessings."

Vann climbed up into the driver's bench of the carriage after having lifted Savannah into her seat. She snuggled up close to him thinking . . . *What a birthday this has been!*

When they got back to Willow Place Savannah realized that she didn't know when Vann's birthday was nor even how old he was, so she inquired, "Vann, when is your birthday?"

"My birthday gets things started off right. It happens to be January first. This upcoming birthday I'll be 25 . . . a quarter of a century old!"

"Then that gives me three months and eleven days to come up with something special for your birthday."

"Yes, and that reminds me, I have a special gift for you." He reached into his vest pocket and handed her a small box. "Go ahead. Open it."

She looked at him suspiciously as she took the box. It was a dark blue velvet box with a snap clasp. She pressed the small pearl clasp and it opened. Inside was a beautiful gold compass with an enamel dial and convex glass. She lifted it from the box. The compass was hanging from a gold chain. It was about an inch-and-a-half in diameter and very dainty. She loved it!

"My dear Savannah, you should never get lost again as long as you wear your compass."

Chapter 13

SEPTEMBER 20TH,
THURSDAY

*M*organ stood on the back platform of the train as it pulled away from the train station. He waved to his father, mother and Savannah. He was on his way back to Williamsburg. It had been a sad goodbye. He almost abandoned his dream when Savannah was lost. But she was fine now and happy with Vann. She would be at home with his parents, so Morgan would proceed with his plan. He and Greg would go to New York and investigate the possibilities there.

As the train rounded the curve and Morgan was out of sight, Elizabeth leaned into Zachary's chest and began to sob, just as she had done when Zachary had left her to go to Williamsburg some 26 years ago. That's when he went to Williamsburg on business for the shipping company and then headed on to Norfolk for a sailboat excursion with his brother, Ben. They were lost at sea in a storm and were blessed to make it through alive. Elizabeth had a foreboding about that trip from the beginning. However, she did not feel the same way about Morgan's leaving. She wasn't worried about his safe return. But she did feel sad that her only son would be so far away.

Zachary embraced her in his strong arms and let her have her cry. Then he said, "Dry your tears now, Elizabeth. Where's your handkerchief?"

Surprisingly, she still had it in her hand and hadn't dropped it. She pressed it to her eyes, then her nose and gave him a weak little smile.

"Elizabeth, this train depot has many wonderful memories for us. We've always referred to it as hallowed ground. I'm not apprehensive about Morgan leaving Richmond. This was his choice. Remember, you made a choice to stay at Willow Place, and you were very adamant about that choice. I think Morgan has quite a bit of your spunk. Let's let him go and be happy for him."

Savannah said, "Bravo, Father, bravo! Mother, Morgan is 24 years old and not your 'little' boy now. He wants to fly and you must give him that freedom. He doesn't need to feel bound by us nor tradition. Remember, I'm the one who loves Willow Place. You don't have to worry about me leaving, ever. And Morgan will be back. Wait and see!"

With her feelings just a little bruised, she accepted these admonitions with courage. After all, Morgan had promised that he would be home for Christmas.

Morgan found when he got back to Williamsburg that Greg had told his parents, Phillip and Jane, of their plans. They were not so surprised because Phillip had overheard Morgan and Greg talking about their plans a couple of months before. He talked to Jane about it but they decided to wait and see if this notion took wings. They were somewhat skeptical about the outcome but felt the boys had their right to explore. Greg did ask them not to tell his sister, Mary Ann, because he knew Morgan would want to tell her himself.

On Saturday, before they were to leave on Monday, Morgan made a date with Mary Ann. They spent the afternoon together attending a sailboat parade on the James River. They both were overwhelmed at the beauty of some of the new sailboat entrees. They were very colorful with sleeker body shapes. It was a perfect day. The sun was bright and the winds were just right for sailing. They both picked out a particular boat as their favorite. It was all white with the name "Hope" emblazoned in deep-sea blue lettering on its side. She won first prize. They left happy. They called it their "hope boat."

"Mary Ann, let's go to the River Restaurant for an early meal. It'll be quiet and cozy there. I have something to talk with you about," Morgan said.

"That sounds great to me. I suddenly realize I'm very hungry," Mary Ann responded as she admired his black hair that had just a hint of curl in it. She wondered what he wanted to talk with her about. Her mind was busy trying to figure it out. It had been four months since he graduated from William and Mary. He had enjoyed a summer of sailing. She knew from their conversation that he was interested in sailing and water adventures to the point of perhaps getting into the shipping business. Also, they had been seeing more and more of each other. Could his interest in her be serious? She would soon find out.

They had finished their meal. It was too early for the evening diners to be there. Their table was in a semi-private area with a nice view of the river and a very relaxed atmosphere.

Mary Ann asked, "So you want to talk with me about something?"

"Yes, Mary Ann, I do. First let me tell you that I've grown very fond of you these last few months. I've always been fond of you seeing how our families have been close all of our lives. But my feelings for you are different now. I hope you share these feelings," he said as he took hold of her hand.

"It goes without saying, Morgan, but exactly what are you getting at?"

This was harder than Morgan had anticipated. He expected a more passionate response.

"I'm going to be leaving Williamsburg this coming Monday. In fact, Greg and I will be leaving together. We're going to New York to look for work opportunities there. I don't know just when we'll be back. If we find the right jobs we won't be coming back to stay any time soon, only for visits. I care enough about you, Mary Ann, to ask you to wait for me."

Mary Ann removed her hand from his. She asked, "What on earth has gotten into you, Morgan? You live in the very best part of the country and you have all kinds of opportunities right here in Williamsburg or certainly in Richmond working with your father. Why New York? Why Yankee country? Have you forgotten The War Between the States? Williamsburg and Richmond didn't fight on the same side in the war as New York. Have you forgotten how long it has taken us to rebuild after that horrible war? I can't believe you're entertaining such a plan, Morgan Bainbridge."

When Mary Ann called him by his first and last name she meant business. When she narrowed her gorgeous brown eyes, Morgan knew he had better tread softly.

"Mary Ann, this is a great nation we live in. I haven't seen all of it that I hope to see. I'll admit that I'm adventurous. The new and unknown appeal to me but I don't consider myself to be foolhardy. I have a business degree and I intend to use it somewhere. It might not be New York, but I must go and see what it offers. It's important to me that you understand."

"Well, I don't. I just don't understand at all. If you think I'm going to sit here at home and wait while you're out exploring then you're mistaken. I will not!" she said through clinched teeth. "And furthermore, I think you and Greg both have lost your minds. To think I had dreamy thoughts of the two of us. Humph!"

So she did care . . . she just said so. She said she had dreamy thoughts of the two of us! Maybe, just maybe, there's still a chance she'll change her mind.

"I had no idea you would be so opposed to this, Mary Ann. Your mother and father have given Greg their blessings and I had so hoped you might feel the same way," Morgan said pleadingly as he reached for her hand again.

She pulled it away and stood to her feet. "Will you please take me home now, Morgan?"

Riding to the Maxwell's in the carriage there wasn't a word spoken. When they arrived, Mary Ann jumped down from the carriage and ran inside.

Again Morgan thought of calling this venture off but he just couldn't. This was something he had to do. He couldn't explain it but he knew he had to go to New York!

Chapter 14

Morgan and Greg had spied out the land in New York for two weeks. They had answered ads in the papers for work opportunities. So far they had not found what they were looking for. Greg had a degree in corporate law. Morgan's degree was in business.

They liked New York, especially the lower Manhattan area, since both were interested in the shipping industry. This area seemed to be the hub of shipping. They noticed a different advertisement in the New York Times. It was set apart from their regular ads. It was bordered in black, very eye catching. The message read:

Prominent shipping firm needs
Business Manager and possibly
Corporate Attorney. Proper
Credentials required.
Bristol Shipping, Inc.
1616 Water Street
Manhattan, N.Y.

Morgan said, "Greg, maybe, just maybe, this is what we've been looking for. It's uncanny they seem to need what the two of us have to offer."

Greg looked the part of an attorney. He was always impeccably dressed. He had the olive complexion of his mother, Jane. His eyes were like those of his father, Phillip, blue as the sky on a cloudless day and his brown hair was very thick and well groomed. A neatly trimmed mustache and an attractive cleft chin gave him a dashing look. But he had an authoritative air about him that demanded respect.

Greg laid down the newspaper and said, "I suggest we hire a carriage and go see these people."

Arriving at the Water Street address, they were impressed by what they saw. They entered a reception area. A gentleman appeared asking if he could assist them.

"We're here to answer this advertisement," Morgan said, flashing the ad from the New York Times.

"Then follow me, gentlemen."

They walked down a long, wide hall with offices on either side. Midway they came to a door marked, Bristol Shipping, Inc., Jordan Bristol, President. When the gentleman opened the door they were surprised at the spaciousness of the place. There were several desks placed tastefully within the large room where men were busily working. The walls had handsome, dark mahogany chair railing, and the upper walls were painted white with a two-foot cornice board trim of carved mahogany. The ceiling was painted the same color as the walls. This made the room very bright and airy. One wall was lined with windows bringing in the outside light. In the center of another wall was an extra large fireplace with a carved mahogany mantle to match the cornice board. In the center of the mantle was a handsome English aneroid barometer of brass and dark mahogany. Above the mantle was an original painting of a Trans Atlantic freighter.

They were escorted to a waiting room. The gentleman knocked lightly on the door, was told to come in, and disappeared, closing the door behind him.

They waited about fifteen minutes before being asked to go into Mr. Bristol's office. While they were waiting Morgan kept thinking, *where have I heard that name, Jordan Bristol, before? It sounds so familiar.*

"Good morning, gentlemen, I'm Jordan Bristol," he said extending his hand. "Please have a seat. So you're here to inquire about our ad in the New York Times? Suppose you tell me about yourself."

"I'm Morgan Bainbridge and this is my friend Greg Maxwell IV. We've graduated from William and Mary College in Williamsburg, Virginia. I have a degree in business administration."

Greg chimed in, "My degree is in corporate law. My father was also an attorney but now teaches at his alma mater, William and Mary, in Williamsburg."

They had quite a lengthy conversation about why they decided to come to New York, focusing on the opportunities to be involved in the shipping industry. Morgan told of his great-grandfather owning and operating Morgan Shipping of Williamsburg for years before selling it. Both admitted to loving the sport of sailing. They expounded on their credentials, adding that both had graduated college with honors.

"We both are acquainted with hard work and are happiest when we are busy," Morgan stated.

During their conversation, Jordan Bristol kept wondering why the name Bainbridge rang such a bell. It wasn't a common name but he knew he'd heard it before. He had to admit he was impressed by these two young men. His shipping business had grown in the last five years. His business manager, Wade Hamilton, was getting ready to step down. He wanted to bring in a fresh young mind for Wade to train before he retired. Also, the laws of shipping were so stringent and the business so competitive that he needed an in-house attorney to deal with the many technical aspects of it.

Mr. Bristol stood to his feet and shook hands with the two of them. He would let them know his decision in a few days.

Chapter 15

Morgan and Greg had been working at Bristol Shipping, Inc. for six weeks. The work had been very rewarding. They both had learned a lot. There was more to shipping than they ever imagined. But with minds like sponges they quickly soaked up everything that was tossed at them. They were pleased with the company and Mr. Bristol, especially. He was a very nice man. They found him to be caring and giving but he demanded everyone's very best effort. He stressed honesty and fairness to his employees.

The Thanksgiving holidays were only four days away. Mr. Bristol knew that Morgan and Greg would not be going south until the Christmas break, so he invited them to have Thanksgiving dinner at his home with his family. They thanked him for his graciousness and accepted the invitation.

The Bristol's lived on Fulton Street in an impressive neighborhood. At the entrance to their house were brick buttresses on either side of a circular driveway that was lined with evergreen shrubs and holly bushes. The house itself was red brick with white columns. Gaslights were placed along the driveway and at the entrance of their home.

Greg whistled between his teeth. "This is quite a place, wouldn't you say, Morgan? Bristol Shipping must make big money."

"I'd say Bristol Shipping is the right place for us to get our feet wet in this shipping world. No doubt about it," Morgan replied.

Higgins, The Bristol's Butler, ushered them to the drawing room. Jordan Bristol awaited them. He stood to his feet and greeted them with a warm handshake.

"The family will be down shortly. Please be seated," Mr. Bristol said.

Immediately a tray with piping hot, spiced apple cider was brought in for their enjoyment. Pleasantries were exchanged. Then Mr. Bristol stood to his feet as his wife entered the room.

"Hannah, this is Morgan Bainbridge and Greg Maxwell, the two young men I've been telling you about. Gentlemen, this is my wife, Hannah."

Hannah extended her hand first to Greg. He stooped over and, bringing her hand to his lips, gave her a southern greeting and said, "Pleased to meet you, Mrs. Bristol."

She took a step toward Morgan also extending her hand. He just stood there, speechless. When the situation became awkward, Hannah dropped her hand to her side.

Morgan regained his composure, reached for her hand and also kissed it.

"Please forgive my rudeness, Mrs. Bristol. It's just that you look so much like my mother I was stunned. Really, I've heard it said that everyone has a twin and you could pass for my mother's twin. You are quite beautiful," Morgan said sincerely.

Jordan Bristol's mind raced back to the entryway of a beautiful Richmond house in 1862 during the Civil War. In his mind he saw this beautiful, raven-haired lady holding a baby in her arms and the hand of a small boy. She looked so much like Hannah that he too was shocked at their resemblance. He remembered being separated from his unit, being dirty and half starved. He and six of his men had stopped by this house and asked for food. The mistress of the house had given them a flour sack of meat, bread and apples. They left hurriedly and back tracked to where they had gotten separated from their unit. He and the other men, out of sheer desperation, attempted to swim to the Union ship, The Galena, but were captured by one Lt. Zachary Bainbridge. So, that is where he had heard the name Bainbridge before. Morgan was that little boy holding to his mother's hand on that sad and fateful day!

Jordan's daughters entered the drawing room and derailed his train of thought.

"Good evening girls. I'd like you to meet two southern gentlemen who are now with Bristol Shipping. This is Greg Maxwell and Morgan Bainbridge. May I present my daughters, Beth Lee and Amy Elizabeth?"

Morgan and Greg rose to their feet when the girls entered.

"Pleased to meet you both," the boys said in unison.

"It's our pleasure," Beth Lee answered.

"Dad has told us good things about both of you. He's a stickler for good work ethics which he says you both have," Amy said, "and he's very impressed with your southern manners."

"Speaking of manners, its good manners that we eat on time with these our special guests," Hannah Bristol said, standing to her feet and leading the way to their formal dining room.

When everyone was seated, Mr. Bristol said, "Let us pray. Our Heavenly Father, we are grateful this Thanksgiving evening to have as our guests around our table young Morgan and Greg. Let them feel a spirit of love in our home and a feeling of welcome. Bless this abundance of food on our table, which thou hast provided. Let us ever be thankful for your blessings each day. Amen. Boys, enjoy the food as though you were around your mother's table at home."

The meal was a traditional Thanksgiving feast served in five courses. To begin with the conversation was somewhat reserved but became less formal as the meal progressed. By the time they retired back to the drawing room for coffee they felt like old friends.

The girls asked lots of questions about the South. The conversation was lively and the evening passed quickly, it seemed, and it was time to say goodnight.

"Well, what did you think, my friend?" Greg asked Morgan.

"These are very nice people. We're fortunate to be working for Jordan Bristol. Indeed they are wealthy people. Their home is a show place." Morgan replied. "Plus, Mrs. Bristol looks enough like my mother to be her twin sister. I've never seen anything like it. Do you agree?"

"Yes, Morgan, their resemblance is quite remarkable, almost too much to be a mere coincidence."

"She even has mannerisms like mother. The way she holds the goblet she drinks from. The gestures she makes when she talks. And those deep dimples in each cheek are identical to mother's. But how could she look so much like mother and not be kin?" Morgan said perplexed.

Chapter 16

After retiring, Jordan Bristol had a lot of thinking to do. Even Morgan Bainbridge saw the strong resemblance of Hannah and his mother, Elizabeth. Jordan knew that Hannah was adopted and so did Hannah. They had joked many times about her being southern born in Charlottesville, Virginia and now was a "Yankee" from New York.

Hannah's parents had been wealthy plantation owners who lived in Charlottesville. They were childless and longed for a baby. After they adopted Hannah they sold their plantation, moved to New York and invested in a shipping company. They would never have felt safe living in the same town as the parents of their daughter, Hannah. The only thing they new about the mother of the baby was that her name was Victoria Sloan and she had given birth to twin girls on November 2, 1836. They really didn't want to know more. As a result, Hannah had lived all of her life in New York. Both of Hannah's parents, Harry and Anna Anderson, were now deceased. They were in their mid-thirty's when they adopted Hannah and were in their mid seventies when they died.

Jordan Bristol went to work for Mr. Anderson in 1850 when he was eighteen. He met Hannah a year later. In February of 1855 they were married. Their first daughter, Beth Lee, was born in January 1856, and Amy Elizabeth in December 1857. Those were good years for the Bristol's and the Anderson's. Jordan had learned the shipping business well and Mr. Anderson depended heavily on him. Then in April 1861, the Civil War broke out. Jordan felt compelled to volunteer for service. In May of 1862 he was captured near Richmond by a Lt. Bainbridge. However, shortly afterwards, he and two of his men were able to escape. They got back to the Union Army and were assigned to another unit. Fortunately he made it through the rest of the war without a scratch.

As the years went by, the Anderson's ceased to worry that Hannah's birth mother might find them and ask for Hannah back. Since they got her the day she was born, she was just like their very own daughter, the Anderson's had told Jordan. From the beginning they had told Hannah that she was adopted. They succeeded in making her feel that she was the most special child in the world.

Jordan had asked Mr. Anderson why the mother had given up one child and kept the other one. Mr. Anderson said the attorney on their case told them the mother had been mistreated by her first husband who was accidentally killed before the babies were born. She had remarried a very caring and loving man who knew of her condition. However, she felt she might loose her husband if she presented him with two daughters to care for as his own. She was emotionally fragile at the time. Under different circumstances her decision might not have been so drastic. But she didn't want her husband to know about the twin birth. She was very concerned that the baby be adopted by loving parents that would give her a good home. The Anderson's were contacted and came immediately for Hannah. Of course, Victoria kept the other child.

Jordan tossed and turned most of the night thinking what he must do about this situation. Should he let sleeping dogs lie? Or should he talk with Hannah about his suspicions. This information, if it were true, would touch a lot of lives and bring about changes. As he saw it, the changes would be good ones. Since Hannah's parents were gone she had no real family. To deny her the knowledge that she had a twin sister would not be right. The night was long and his thoughts worrisome.

The morning sun finally shined through the breakfast room where Jordan was sitting. He had been up since long before daybreak. It was the day after Thanksgiving and he wouldn't be going into the office. He had been talking to the Lord about his suspicions, asking His guidance concerning the matter. He knew he needed Godly wisdom if he were to discuss things with Hannah. The book of Proverbs was a good source for direction in life. He turned to the 15th chapter and read randomly. Verse 4 said, "A wholesome tongue is a tree of life:" Then his eyes fell on verse 23, which really did speak to him. "A man hath joy by the answer of his mouth: and a word spoken in due season, how good is it!" Reading on, he turned to chapter 16, verse 9. "A man's heart deviseth his way: but the Lord directeth his steps." He finished with verse 20. "He that handleth a matter wisely shall find good: and whoso trusteth in the Lord, happy is he." He breathed a prayer of thanksgiving and felt that he had his answer. These blessed old scriptures seemed to say that it was alright to tell Hannah what he suspected, that it was the only thing to do.

"Good morning, Jordan," Hannah said as she entered the breakfast room. "You didn't rest well last night, dear. Was something troubling you?"

"Just how did you know that I didn't rest well?" he asked, rising to his feet and greeting her with a kiss.

"You must have turned over a dozen times and then you got up early. Maybe you ate too much Thanksgiving dinner last evening."

"No, that wasn't it. I had a reason for not resting well. Let's eat breakfast and then we'll talk."

"I only want coffee and a bran muffin, Jordan. What would you like?"

"I'd like the same, except maybe two muffins. Those bran muffins smell delicious."

After breakfast they went into a small sitting room off the breakfast room where there was a warm fire in the fireplace. They settled into their favorite chairs, both watching the flames dance in the fireplace.

"Hannah, I have some suspicions I want to talk with you about. I believe you'll be receptive to them. I don't believe they will be harmful to you, in fact, quite the contrary. I believe they will be a blessing. Bear with me as I share them with you."

When Jordan had finished with his story he searched her face for her reaction. It didn't take him long to get his answer.

"Jordan, this is wonderful! Suppose it's true. Just suppose that I do have a twin sister. How can we know for sure?"

"With your permission I intend to talk with Morgan and tell him what I've told you. He would know the name of his mother's mother. If it's Victoria Sloan then we'll know the truth. And if she's still alive you can finally meet your birth mother, if she will agree to it. Also, you can meet your twin sister. That would mean that Morgan Bainbridge is your nephew and his sister, Savannah, would be your niece. Beth Lee and Amy will have gained a whole new family."

"Suppose Morgan isn't interested in our pursuing this, then what?" Hannah asked.

"I feel sure Morgan will feel exactly as we do about this matter. Also, we'll need to talk with Beth Lee and Amy. We can do that at lunch today," Jordan said.

When Jordan told the girls the whole story they were so excited they said it seemed like Christmas had come early.

"Wouldn't you know it . . . just when I had my eye on Morgan I'd find out he just might be my *cousin*! My, my," Amy declared.

MONDAY, NOVEMBER 26TH.

Jordan went into Morgan's office shortly after arriving. Morgan had papers spread out all over his desktop and was hard at work. Tenderness spread over Jordan as he looked at this fine young man and thought; *if it turns out that he isn't Hannah's nephew, what a disappointment it will be.*

"Just one moment, Mr. Bristol, and I'll be right with you," Morgan said as he looked up. "I'm almost finished checking the paperwork on this shipment that leaves in a couple of hours for Europe. Accuracy on this shipment is vital. I'll have Mr. Hamilton check my final figures to make sure there's no problem."

Morgan continued diligently as though the president of the company was not waiting to talk with him! Jordan appreciated the maturity Morgan was showing in his detailed work ethics. He sat down, leaned back in the chair and smiled at his good fortune in finding Morgan and Greg to come on board with Bristol Shipping Company.

Chapter 17

*L*et me run this over to Mr. Hamilton's office. I'll be right back, Morgan said as he hurriedly walked out the door.

Returning, he reached out and shook hands with Jordan and then said, "What brings you into my office so early, Mr. Bristol?"

"You better sit down for this, Morgan. It'll take a while."

When Jordan had finished Morgan looked very thoughtful. He'd said very little but had listened intently. Morgan had a way of hiding his emotions when he deemed it necessary.

"I don't have to tell you, Mr. Bristol, this is quite perplexing. It's a lot to digest, so many unanswered questions. I hardly feel at liberty to discuss this further without first speaking with my mother. I hope you understand."

"I do understand. I've had several days to ponder this and you've only just learned the suspicions. I must tell you that Hannah and the girls are very excited that they might have a whole new family, for what it might be worth to you."

"As you already know, Greg and I were hoping to go home for Christmas. But with this information I'm wondering if I should make a trip back to Richmond now. Such suspicions need to be addressed immediately, wouldn't you agree?" Morgan asked thoughtfully.

"Yes, I wholeheartedly agree. There's no reason why you can't leave immediately. Wade can handle any business here that needs attention. It's 9:30 now. There will be a 10:30 A.M. train going south. If you hurry you should be able to make connections."

"I'll do that. I should be back ready to start work by Friday afternoon. I can burn some midnight oil and work Saturday to catch up somewhat," Morgan said as he stood to his feet.

"The end of the year is not a real busy time in shipping, Morgan. Take your time. Give your family our warm regards," Jordan said shaking hands with young Morgan Bainbridge.

Morgan arrived in Richmond Tuesday afternoon about 4:00 P.M. He took a carriage from the train depot to his father's office. He knocked on the door before opening it.

Without looking up his father said, "Yes, what is it?"

"Would you stop long enough to welcome your son home?" Morgan said, with a smile in his voice.

"Morgan! What are you doing here? Come in son, come in. What a pleasant surprise. I hope there's nothing wrong. Is there?" Zachary asked hesitantly.

"Well, yes and no. Wrong? Perhaps not. But I had to come home to find out. I must talk with you, father. Can you call it a day now? I have a lot of territory to cover and only a short time to cover it in," Morgan said with a serious look on his face.

"We can leave right now. I suppose that you want to go home. Your mother will be surprised as well as Savannah. We didn't expect to see you back here until Christmas."

"Nor did I expect to come back before Christmas, but something urgent has come up that needs the family's attention. I'll fill you in on our ride home. I wanted to talk with you before I talk to mother."

Elizabeth and Savannah were in the parlor working on needlepoint. They both had become very proficient in this art. It was evidenced by needlepoint pillow tops that had been made into cushions and spread over the house as well as table runners on various tables throughout their home. Savannah's favorite was an exquisite wall hanging displayed in the library. It had been on display in the Richmond Museum of Art. The museum had invited local artists to submit their work for approval to be placed there for one month. Savannah's wall hanging had been selected.

The two were so engrossed in their work they did not hear Zachary and Morgan come in.

"Is this the greeting a prodigal son receives upon his return, may I ask?" Morgan said in a mock, hurt voice.

"Morgan, Morgan!" Savannah shrieked as she jumped up, spilling her needlepoint onto the floor and darting toward him. She hugged and patted him and repeated his name again!

"Well now, that's more like it, little sister."

Elizabeth laid her needlepoint aside and waited her turn for Morgan's embrace.

"My son, what a joy it is to see you. We didn't expect you until Christmas. What has brought you home early?" Elizabeth inquired, as she lovingly touched his handsome face.

"Something urgent has come up that I need to discuss with the family, mother," he answered, as he gave her a warm hug and kiss. "But first I've been on the train since yesterday morning at 10:30. I need a bath and a change of clothing. Then I could stand some of Rosie's good food," Morgan explained as he walked toward the door to go upstairs to his room.

"If we had known in time we would have killed the fatted calf," Savannah yelled as he took the steps two at a time.

"Zachary, is there something wrong?" Elizabeth asked with a concerned look on her face. "What on earth could have brought Morgan here just a month before he would be coming for the Christmas holidays? It must be something serious."

"We shall see in just a short while, dear. The important thing is to tell Rosie to set another plate at the dinner table for Morgan. See if she has time to bake a dark chocolate cake with that special white frosting that Morgan loves so much. We could have that as a late dessert," Zachary said as he went to freshen up for dinner.

Chapter 18

After dinner they retired to the library. Morgan was glad to be home. The familiar surroundings enveloped him with warmth. Willow Place was a place of beauty and comfort . . . beauty because God's handiwork was very evident all around the grounds . . . comfort because his wonderful parents had made it so. To him and Savannah it was a safe haven. He had never appreciated it more than now.

He turned to his mother who was sitting next to him and asked, "Mother, do you remember that time during the civil war when Union troops came to our home and demanded food? I know you recorded it in one of your journals. Could you find it and read it?"

She walked to the bookcase behind the big desk, selected a journal and began to turn the pages and read:

. . . May 17, 1862 - Part of this ugly war has come to our beloved Willow Place. Some tired and dirty Union soldiers stormed up on our porch pounding on the front door. Molly

Thatcher answered their rude knocking. As they pushed their way into the foyer I approached them from the parlor. Morgan was holding my hand and I was carrying avannah. It was evident that the man in front of the group was an officer of the Union army. Upon seeing me, he turned white in the face and took two steps backward. For a moment he was speechless. He regained his composure quickly.

"Are you the mistress of the house?" he asked almost gently.

I nodded my head yes.

"I'm Lieutenant Jordan Bristol . . ."

Before Elizabeth could continue Morgan said, "That's enough, mother. You can stop there. We all remember the story very well as we've shared in your wonderful journals many times. I must tell you that the man I'm working for is this same man, Jordan Bristol. He's the owner of Bristol Shipping Company, Inc. in lower Manhattan. He's one of the finest men I've ever met."

"This is certainly surprising, Morgan. But I can't see why you felt you needed to come home to tell me this."

"There's a lot more to the story, mother. Be patient and I'll tell you what I found out on Monday morning at 9:30. This is what prompted me to catch the 10:30 train that same morning to come to Richmond."

When he had finished there was a hush in the room. Elizabeth was a strong person. She did not bend under pressure as a rule. She thought things through, prayerfully, and then reacted to the situation accordingly. Was this news shocking to her? Of course it was. But a mental picture began to form in her mind. She was 44 years old. She had lost every member of her immediate family; first her father, whom she had never known because he had died six months before she was born. Her mother had died when she was four, so she had very little memory of her. Both sets of grandparents were gone. She could hardly comprehend that she might have a twin sister. A brother-in-law and two nieces, as well, meant she would have a brand new family. She had nothing to lose in this venture, but oh so much to gain!

All eyes were upon her, she realized. They had been polite enough to wait until she spoke before saying anything themselves.

"Morgan, you are a faithful son. I'm so thankful that you came home to tell me such wonderful news. Yes, *it is wonderful news*. I can barely comprehend it," Elizabeth exclaimed.

Savannah was giddy with excitement and questions. Zachary was taking all of this in with a smile on his face. Morgan was so relieved he felt almost drained. He hadn't realized the pressure he'd been under.

"Morgan, did you tell the Bristol's that my mother's name was Victoria Sloan?" Elizabeth asked her son.

"No mother. When they told me her name, I decided I needed to come home and talk with you before I told them anything. But I KNEW. I knew right then that you and she were sisters. I could have gotten very excited. I cannot convey to you what nice people the Bristol's are. Granted, they are very wealthy, but they're the salt-of-the-earth type people. They seem to have high Christian principles. And, Hannah's parents who raised her were southerners. Both of them were born and raised in Virginia. Beth Lee and Amy are well-mannered ladies. I can see a likeness in Amy and Savannah. Beth Lee resembles her father, Jordan. I could not be working for a more stable company or for a better man than Mr. Bristol. You know, we are going to have to make some changes in what we call people. I can't go back to work and call Uncle Jordan Mr. Bristol!"

They all laughed. Rosie did get the chocolate cake baked and they were served in the library. Morgan had a giant slice of the cake. They talked some more about this newfound family. Finally, Morgan told them he would have only tomorrow to spend with them before he had to head back to New York on Thursday morning. He excused himself and retired for the night.

Chapter 19

Wednesday was spent making plans. Elizabeth said she would send an invitation to the Bristol's to come to Willow Place for the Christmas holidays. Just five years ago Elizabeth and Zachary had part of the house redesigned. Zachary's parents and family from Norfolk were frequent visitors as well as Phillip and Jane Maxwell and children. They now had four bedrooms downstairs, each having its own water closet. This added space would insure the Bristol's a comfortable visit. Morgan felt sure the Bristol's would accept the invitation to come. Excitement filled the Bainbridge house!

In the afternoon Morgan and Savannah went horseback riding. They rode all over Willow Place and drank in its beauty. A lot could be said about rural living as opposed to city living. Morgan realized just how much he had missed the wide-open spaces.

He asked Savannah, "How has the family worked out that bought grandfather Morgan's house up on the hill?"

"They are fine people. We hardly know they're there. As you know, for such a long time, mother couldn't bear to have anyone live there after grandfather and grandmother died. But the place is so beautiful she hated to have it stand empty. When the Lee Dyer family approached mother about buying the place, mother decided it was time to let it go. As you remember they moved in the year before you left for college. Mother did stipulate that if they ever decided to sell she would buy it back."

Morgan and Savannah decided to ride into Richmond and have a sandwich at The Sandwich Shop, one of their favorite places.

"Alright, little sister, tell me what's going on with you and Vann Baker? I haven't heard his name mentioned since I've been here, but I might add, it's only been 24 hours. I know how fond you are of him. How has the relationship progressed?"

"He has asked me to marry him, Morgan, and I said yes. We haven't set a date yet, but it will probably be this next spring. I've talked it over with mother and father. Vann has talked with his parents, but we haven't made a public engagement announcement as yet. We love each other so much that we aren't ready to share our deep feelings with others. Does that make any kind of sense to you, Morgan?"

"It does. There's nothing wrong with savoring this special love you have for one another. For you Savannah, I think it's a sweet, magical time and belongs only to the two of you. When you set the date then you can shout it from the roof tops!"

"Oh Morgan, I knew you would understand. You always do understand me, even when others don't. Vann is my friend. We share the same interests. It's important to us both to settle down right here in this area. I could not bear to leave Willow Place, to be where I couldn't ride over the spread and enjoy its beauty. Vann and I can sit and talk for hours, never tiring of each other's company. At other times we sit quietly, listening to the sounds around us. There's no need for words. We are truly kindred spirits."

"Savannah, it pleases me to see you so happy. Your welfare is very important to me. If Vann makes you this happy, then he's got to be an alright fellah. I only wish things in my life were on track. Right now they seem to be derailed," Morgan said, with a hint of despair.

"Why, Morgan. What on earth do you mean?"

"It's a long story, Sis, but to sum it up, I'm very much in love with Mary Ann Maxwell. This should not come as a surprise to you or the family. But she was very opposed to my going to New York. Right now she isn't speaking to me. I wish I had time to go on to Williamsburg to see her before going back to New York. However, I really must get back by Friday afternoon. I plan to work late Friday night, and then on Saturday to catch up on paperwork that will have stacked up since I've been gone. So it'll have to wait until the Christmas holidays," Morgan said with a far away look in his eyes.

"I'm not surprised that you're in love with Mary Ann. We've all suspected that you two would eventually get married. I know that she loves you. Given time she'll make the right decision. If she loves you as I love Vann, she'll come to realize that without you she won't be happy anywhere," Savannah stated emphatically. "By the way, have you written her since you've been in New York?"

"Yes, I've written her eight letters but haven't heard a word. I was so sure of my feelings for her that I took for granted that she felt the same way about me. If she doesn't, now is the best time to find out."

"May I make a suggestion, Morgan? Don't write her again. Let her go for three weeks without hearing from you. By Christmas I feel she'll be more than glad to see you."

"It's worth a try. I can put to a test the old saying 'absence makes the heart grow fonder.' It's already worked for me," Morgan said with a sigh.

Chapter 20

Morgan had a good trip back to New York. He'd been able to sleep well in the Pullman Thursday night. He arrived back at the office at 4:30 P.M. on Friday. Jordan was still there. Morgan tapped lightly on his office door that was slightly open, walked inside and said, "Good afternoon, Uncle Jordan!"

Jordan stood up at once, walked around his desk and gave Morgan a big handshake and then embraced him, exclaiming, "Then it's true? Hannah and your mother are really sisters?"

"Yes, it's true. It was an exciting visit. Mother is ecstatic at the prospects of meeting her newfound sister as well as all of you. Father and Savannah are all smiles as well. Mother is sending a written invitation for you to spend Christmas at Willow Place if you don't have other plans already," Morgan said.

"Wild horses couldn't keep us from going. I know you came to the office to work, but Wade Hamilton has been right on top of things since you've been gone. Even Greg has pitched in to take up the slack. I explained to both of them why you left so suddenly to go home. Both are anxious to hear the outcome. But I've said all of that to say let's go home and tell the good news to Hannah and the girls. Greg is already planning to be there for dinner this evening."

"Are you sure it's alright for me to leave? I came prepared to burn some midnight oil," Morgan stated.

"Come on, nephew, time's wasting! We've waited for this news since Monday."

As they walked through the large outer office and down the hall, there was a great feeling of camaraderie between the two of them.

"You mentioned Greg would be coming for dinner tonight. I'm glad. I want him to be in on this good news," Morgan explained.

"By all means. And I might add that he and Beth Lee have become interested in one another. She has finally found someone who challenges her," Jordan replied, shaking his head affirmatively.

After dinner the six of them gathered in the sitting room. All eyes were on Morgan as he began to tell them about his trip home.

Chapter 21

DECEMBER 21, 1880

The air was filled with excitement and anticipation as the Jordan Bristol Family, Morgan Bainbridge and Greg Maxwell awaited the arrival of the train in New York that would take them south to Richmond, Virginia. The Christmas holidays had finally arrived and Hannah Bristol, now 44, was going to meet her twin sister, Elizabeth Bainbridge, for the very first time.

The Christmas spirit prevailed as a church youth choir sang Christmas carols at the New York Central station as passengers were coming in. This had been a tradition for this particular church for several years. People had come to expect it.

Soft snowflakes were falling. The ladies were bundled up in their snug-fitting coats and colorful bonnets, some trimmed in white fur framing their faces. The hustle and bustle of the people in the large train station, arms loaded with gifts for family they were going to visit, added to the charm of the season.

The train arrived at 10:30 A.M., right on time. The incoming passengers stepped off the train, some into the awaiting arms of loved ones. Others were calling the names of faces they saw farther down the platform and waving as they walked hurriedly toward them.

"All aboard!" the conductor called out when the platform had cleared of incoming passengers.

Finally they were all aboard and seated. The steam hissed from the big engine as it began to gain speed. The familiar sound of the train rumbling over the tracks was very rhythmic.

Morgan was seated next to Amy. They had become the best of friends. She was very curious about her newfound family. Morgan was careful not to discuss anything he thought should be his mother's right to tell the Bristol's. He knew she would want to tell his Aunt Hannah about their father, John Lee Morgan; also about how she came to meet their grandparents, John and Catherine Morgan. Certainly his mother would want the privilege of telling Hannah all about their mother, Victoria, and their Baldwin grandparents.

"You haven't told us very much about your Willow Place, Morgan. I know I'll be seeing it shortly, but describe it to me," Amy said.

Morgan did his best to draw a mental picture of the place where he grew up. He described it in detail during the spring; the time he thought it was the prettiest. He finished by saying that his mother would not trade it for a king's palace.

The evening meal in the dining car was more delicious than they had expected. Their spirits were running high. Beth Lee and Amy were chatterboxes. They could hardly wait to get to Richmond.

Their accommodations in the Pullman for the night were comfortable. Morgan lay for the longest time wondering about Mary Ann. He had not written her in the last three weeks, nor had he heard from her. Had he lost her completely? Would she see him when he went to Williamsburg? He felt his nagging need to go to New York was somehow directed by a Higher Power, especially in light of what had happened. Would she understand after she found out about Hannah and his mother? So many questions to be answered!

Hannah was so excited she could not go to sleep. The last three weeks had seemed an eternity. She knew she was in for the treat of her life, to have an extended family of her very own flesh and blood.

"Jordan, can you imagine the anticipation I'm experiencing? It's overwhelming. Sometimes I feel that I might be dreaming!" Hannah confided, as she lay with her head on his shoulder.

"I'm almost as excited as you are, Hannah. You and the girls have been my only family for a long time now. I feel that I'll be gaining a lot from this extended family. We all will, no doubt about it," Jordan responded. "We need to try to get some sleep. Tomorrow will be a long day."

Chapter 22

The train pulled into the station in Richmond at 4:00 P.M. on Saturday. This train depot was not as large as the one in New York but it was a busy place this holiday season. Standing on the platform, waiting for baggage, Morgan spied Bart and Jim from Willow Place. Bart was there to pick up their baggage and Jim had come in the big sleigh to carry them home. It had snowed four inches in the last 24 hours. The sleigh was pulled by two big Clydesdales adorned with silver-trimmed harnesses. The sleigh had bells attached to it creating a jingle as they rode along. Jim had done his best to add some magic to the occasion!

Greg had continued on the train to Williamsburg to join his family for Christmas. He would rejoin the Bristol's and Morgan in Richmond after the holidays.

The snow had stopped earlier that morning but the air was crisp and cold. Lap robes made them feel toasty warm as they sat close together. The ride in the open air was exhilarating.

They turned off the main road into the brick-columned entrance to Willow Road.

As they approached the lake and saw the afternoon sun glistening on the snow-laden branches of the willow trees, they gasped at the beauty they beheld. The red berries of the plentiful holly bushes peeped through the snow adding color to the landscape.

The sleigh stopped in front of Willow Place. Morgan noticed the traditional large wreaths tied with red satin bows that hung in every window across the front of the house. On either side of the wreaths were lighted candles. The heavy wooden door had a matching wreath except this one was larger. These familiar decorations made his heart beat a little faster. He was glad to be home for Christmas!

Morgan opened the door, stepped aside, bowed to the Bristol's and said, "Welcome to the Bainbridge home!"

He ushered them into the library where his father, mother and Savannah were awaiting their arrival.

When they got inside the door of the library, Morgan, Jordan, Beth Lee and Amy all stopped and stood very still. Zachary and Savannah stood in complete silence. Elizabeth took a few steps toward Hannah who had walked toward Elizabeth and stopped. They were astonished at what they saw. It was as if they were looking in a mirror. As a matter of fact, they all were astonished.

Finally, Zachary said, "Well girls, you couldn't look more alike if you were twins!"

They all laughed at his joke, which broke the spell. Elizabeth and Hannah hugged each other, cried happy tears, drew back, looked at each other again and hugged some more. Then all of them were hugging each other, exchanging names, calling each other cousin, aunt and uncle, laughing and crying all at the same time. It was a glorious family reunion, free of any pretension and filled with a bonding love.

Sunday morning, December 23rd

Even though it was December 23rd, Elizabeth and Hannah isolated themselves and spent the day reasoning out their past. Hannah was full of questions trying to get a sense of the family she never got to know. Elizabeth went back as far as she could remember and described each of the people who were dear to her heart, beginning with her "Dandy" Baldwin and her Grandmother Savannah. Elizabeth told Hannah about how her grandmother read her very favorite story, "Mary Had a Little Lamb," to her each morning. Hannah exclaimed it was *her* favorite also as a little girl. They discovered they both liked and disliked the same foods, and that their favorite color was green. Both had married tall, blonde men. Hannah had named her first born, Beth Lee, Lee being her Grandfather Baldwin's middle name and certainly not known to her. She named her second born Amy Elizabeth, not knowing she had a twin sister by the name of Elizabeth. The name Hannah was contained in the name Savannah. And the list went on and on. These comparisons had been fun for them.

Elizabeth related the story that had been told to her about their mother Victoria's broken heart after the death of her beloved Alex. She showed Hannah the valentine Alex had made for their mother on their first Valentine's Day dated February 14, 1837. Its words were taken from the Song of Solomon. It was kept inside Victoria's Bible that was now very old.

Elizabeth explained that when Alex died in a fall from his horse, their mother packed their clothes and only a few small items and they came to live at Willow Place with the Baldwin's, Victoria's parents. Elizabeth still had their mother's dresser set, a silver-trimmed hand mirror, hairbrush and comb with a pair of matching silver toilet boxes, all very ornate. These were displayed in a late Victorian, glass curio cabinet in the library along with Victoria's Bible and a few other treasures.

"It seems that our mother's favorite treasure was the wooden box you see there," Elizabeth said, pointing to a mahogany box inside the cabinet. "Let me take it out so you may see it better."

She carefully lifted it and held it in her hands. The top was painted with dainty, gold leaves. When she raised the top there was a velvet-lined compartment that held three jeweled combs Victoria had worn in her hair from time to time. There was also a small drawer with a handle, but it appeared to be a mock drawer that would not open.

"There is a curious story about this box. Grandmother Savannah said the last days of mother's life she asked that the box be placed on the table beside her bed. Mother would fasten her eyes on the box for ever so long. Grandmother said that just hours before she died, Victoria kept saying 'look in the box' in a voice so low it was only audible if you leaned over her bed. Grandmother looked in the box but only found the combs. This seemed to cause Victoria stress. After our mother died, grandmother placed the box in this cabinet where it has remained."

"Do you mind if I hold it?" Hannah asked.

"Of course not. It really is a beautiful piece of heavy mahogany and well-crafted," Elizabeth said, as she handed it to Hannah.

In the exchange, Elizabeth turned the box loose before Hannah had grasped it and it fell to the floor. The top went in one direction, the combs in another and it seemed the bottom had broken open.

Hannah placed her hand over her mouth and her eyes were filled with a look of horror.

"What've I done? I'm so sorry! So very sorry!"

She stooped down and began to gather up the pieces, almost in tears.

"It wasn't your fault, Hannah. I turned the box loose before you had it in your hand. Really, I did! Please don't feel badly," Elizabeth said as she retrieved the bottom half of the box that had dropped at her feet.

"What is this? There is a letter wedged in this part of the box. The box isn't broken at all. Let me see the part you're holding, Hannah. See, this is a drawer. What we always thought was a mock drawer was a real drawer! It was just stuck together. The jar of the box hitting the floor caused it to come out."

They both stared at the letter in the drawer. It fit so snugly it was hard to remove. Elizabeth walked over to the desk and got a letter opener. Sliding it under the letter, carefully, she was able to lift it out. The front was addressed to "Father, Mother and Elizabeth."

Elizabeth and Hannah walked over to the sofa in front of the fireplace, sat down very close together with Elizabeth still holding the letter. They stared at it, realizing the letter was 40 years old and was written by their mother. Elizabeth broke the seal and took out two sheets of stationery folded together. It had yellowed but was in good condition, otherwise. Almost reverently she unfolded the pages. The penmanship was noticeably shaky but dainty and beautiful. Elizabeth began to read aloud.

Dear Father, Mother, and Elizabeth,

I've carried a very heavy secret for the last four years, one I've not shared with anyone, not even my beloved Alex.

You see, on November 2, 1836, I gave birth to twin daughters. Elizabeth, you have a little sister somewhere in this big world we live in.

I gave one of my babies up for adoption. It was a deplorable mistake. At the time I was frightened. I was afraid Alex would not accept two babies to raise that were not his. I know now that he would have accepted you both. After John Lee's death, Alex was there for me, even though he knew I was expecting at the time. Because the accident, which took John Lee's life, happened in Alex's hotel, he came to my rescue.

I thought I had no one else to turn to. If I had gotten in touch with you, my beloved parents, things would've been different. I know now that I should have. But John Lee's mistreatment of me shattered my self esteem and my reasoning powers.

Alex's compassion for me turned to love which I desperately needed. Still being very fragile of spirit, when the doctor told me I had two babies, I panicked. I thought the only answer was to find a good home for one of you. The doctor handled everything. I never saw the baby that was adopted out. I was paid no money. I did not sell my baby.

Alex helped to nurture me back to health, but the enormity of what I'd done hung heavily over me. Then, when Alex was killed in the fall from his horse, my world came crashing down around me.

Not only have I grieved over Alex but over the precious baby I abandoned. The longing for this child will not leave me. I don't have the courage to tell you this in person, but I've written this letter so you may know my secret. I've asked

God over and over to forgive me. Now I ask that you three will forgive me also. I'm truly sorry for all the grief I've put you through. You, Father and Mother, have loved me with an unconditional love which I haven't deserved.

Elizabeth, you will not understand this letter now, but someday you will. Not only have I robbed myself of the love of this other daughter but I have robbed you of a precious sister. I don't have the will to live under the circumstances. I'm placing this letter in the mahogany box that Alex gave to me where I know you'll find it.

Your loving daughter and mother,
Victoria

Chapter 23

Elizabeth and Hannah sat in silence for a few minutes. Elizabeth was only four when her mother died, so she really had very little memory of her. She had already shared with Hannah the whole story of Victoria's life as it had been told to her.

They each wiped a tear away after seeing into the heart of their troubled mother so many years ago. No wonder she kept looking at the box before she died and asked that her own mother look inside.

"Being parents ourselves we can imagine what guilt mother felt over the unfortunate decision she made to give you up for adoption," Elizabeth said sadly. "It could have been me as well as you. No doubt the nurse picked up one of us to give to your parents, leaving the other there for mother."

"I feel sad that I was not raised with you, Elizabeth, and that I never got to know my extended family. But I can say I've had a wonderful life. My father and mother were all I could have asked for. I never felt deprived. Surprisingly, I never wondered about my real mother. I felt complete with my parents. My father's name was Harry and my mother's name was Anna. My name was a combination of their names. There never was a doubt in my mind that they loved me as their very own flesh and blood. If Mother Victoria could see me today, she would see that I was not harmed nor deprived by her actions. I wish she could have known this," Hannah mused.

"So do I. My 'Dandy' often told me that people make their own prisons by poor choices, by not counting the cost of their actions. I'm afraid our mother made poor choices and had to suffer the consequences. She seemed to be an unhappy soul most of her adult life. But in spite of you losing her at birth, and me at the age of four, we have both had happy productive lives thanks to those who lovingly raised us in the fear of the Lord. Since we've finally been brought together, by divine intervention, we should make the most of the years we have left together," Elizabeth said.

"I agree with you, Elizabeth. And I also believe that God sent Morgan to us so we could be brought together. We've never seen Beth Lee and Amy as happy as they've been since they found out they have an extended family. How ironic that Beth 'Lee' was given a family name as well as Amy 'Elizabeth.' Jordan was so impressed with Morgan when he hired him and Greg to go to work at Bristol Shipping. Now that he knows Morgan is his nephew, it's as if he has found a son!"

"We have spent the day away from the family and it has certainly been a profitable time. But this is the holiday season and we need to join them. Let's lay all of this aside and celebrate the spirit of this blessed Christmas season," Elizabeth said as she stood up, locked arms with Hannah and led her toward the sitting room to join the rest of the family.

The morning dawned bright and beautiful. The snow would be melting even more today. The breakfast table was abuzz with chatter, many talking at the same time, just like a big family. Plans were being laid for the day's activities.

To begin with, they all attended Sunday morning church services. The Bristol's were made to feel welcome at First Wesleyan. Pastor David Autry's message was simply titled "Love." He read from the second chapter of Luke expounding on God's love in sending His only Son as a gift for salvation to the whole world. This was the greatest gift ever given and was born out of love for his creation. He ended his message reading from Matthew 2:11, "And when they were come into the house, they saw the young child with Mary his mother, and fell down and worshipped him: and when they had opened their treasures, they presented unto him gifts; gold frankincense, and myrrh."

Continuing on with his message he said, "I see this as the beginning of gift-giving at Christmas, and it, too, was born out of love for a Savior. Sharing gifts with those we love is simply carrying on the tradition that was started back then. The value of the gift is not measured by what someone pays for it, not at all. One of my most treasured gifts came to me wrapped in brown paper and tied with a string. Inside was a piece of beautiful blue glass my seven-year-old daughter had dug up from the yard that had been there for years, no doubt. She has a collection of glass shards she has found and this one was her favorite. I treasure this gift from her heart. Giving is sanctioned throughout the Bible. Remember, God loveth a cheerful giver."

The service ended with the congregation singing "Joy to the World." They all left the service with a feeling of warmth and with giving hearts.

Vann Baker's family had invited the Bainbridge family and their guest over for afternoon cake and coffee. They had become good friends since Vann and Savannah had been seeing each other, and the Baker's wanted to meet Elizabeth's newfound family.

Vann was the oldest son of Chuck and Margaret Baker. Clint, their younger son, was 23. These boys were true cowboys. They loved their horse farm and the outdoor work that went with the territory. They wore boots and Stetsons and walked with an air of confidence.

After Amy met Clint, during the chatter of introductions and hand shaking, she whispered to Savannah as she rolled her eyes, "My, my, my! Is he real?"

"Very real, my dear cousin," she whispered back.

After finishing the refreshments the atmosphere was very relaxed. Vann stood and said, "Mr. and Mrs. Bainbridge, I have a question for you. I'm asking for your daughter's hand in marriage. I love her with all my heart. I want to take care of her for the rest of our lives. I've asked her to marry me and she has said yes. All we need now are your blessings. Do we have them?"

There was a hush over the entire room. Zachary stood as did Elizabeth. They looked at each other and then at this young daughter of theirs. Elizabeth nodded her head yes to Zachary and he spoke.

"We give you two our blessings, and may we be the first to congratulate you. We have become very fond of you, Vann. We believe we can trust Savannah to your care."

Everyone extended heartfelt congratulations and best wishes. Hugs and pats on the back were plentiful.

Amy had stars in her eyes as she exclaimed, "To become engaged on Christmas Eve is the most romantic thing I've heard of! And have you noticed that Savannah contains the name Vann? How interesting!"

"We've always wanted a daughter," Margaret said. "Vann has done us proud in choosing Savannah to be his wife."

"I'd say Savannah is about the purtiest little filly around these parts. You've done well to rope her and pull her in, Son," Chuck said with a wink and a nod of the head.

This was a very typical response from Chuck. Everyone who knew him was aware of his humor. He thought the highest compliment he could pay anyone was to liken them to one of his prize horses.

This was a Christmas Eve that would not soon be forgotten.

Christmas morning found the Bainbridge's and their guests gathered around the gaily decorated, huge, blue spruce Christmas tree in the parlor. The family Bible was opened to the second chapter of Luke. Zachary began reading. Then they took turns reading through verses thirty-three. Savannah began playing "Hark the Herald Angels Sing" on the piano and they all joined in singing the wonderful old Christmas carol.

Elizabeth announced that it was time to open presents. They were like children waiting for their names to be called out. There was an array of scarves, mittens, gloves, socks, sweaters and toboggans exchanged between them.

Rosie served up a feast for their Christmas meal. Vann came calling in the late afternoon and brought Clint along which put a sparkle in Amy's eyes. The whole family went caroling with the church group to West Richmond Hospital. They all agreed this was the right thing to do when they saw the overwhelming pleasure it brought to the patients. Christmas of 1880 was like no other. All of their lives had been changed for the better. Zachary told Elizabeth that love was never in short supply if people would open their hearts to receive it. God had surely provided a miracle in their lives.

Chapter 24

Tuesday morning, December 26th Morgan was on the first train out of Richmond to Williamsburg. He simply had to get some answers from Mary Ann. Greg was expecting him and would be at the train depot to pick him up. He had enjoyed being with the family but it was good to have some time alone. While he was in New York he had buried himself in his work, wanting to learn everything he possibly could about the shipping business. But he missed Mary Ann terribly. He would love for her to come to New York as his wife. What if she wouldn't? Well, he would soon find out.

Greg picked him up just as he said he would. When they were settled in the carriage Greg handed Morgan a wrapped Christmas present.

"What's this?" Morgan inquired.

"I haven't the slightest idea. Why don't you open it and we'll both know!" Greg replied.

The package was about six inches long and four inches wide.

"Who's it from?" Morgan asked.

"Morgan! Open the gift."

"Alright, alright," he replied as he loosened the ribbon of blue and removed the blue, silver and white Christmas paper from the package. Inside was a white box. He lifted the lid and was shocked at what he saw. Then he began to laugh and laugh and said, "Well I'll be!" over and over again.

"Look, I know this is a personal gift but could you just give me a hint what this is all about," Greg prodded.

"If it means what I think it means, Mary Ann does care for me, Greg my boy! Here, just take a look," Morgan said as he handed Greg the box.

Greg looked inside with a puzzled look on his face. "I see here a watercolor of a white sailboat with the word HOPE painted on the hull in blue lettering, which I'm assuming is the name of the sailboat. So where's the message that Mary Ann cares for you? Besides, how do you know it's from Mary Ann?" Greg asked.

"Oh, but it would have to be. The last time I was with Mary Ann we went to a sailboat show. They had some new models in the water. One sailboat that stood out to us was white and sleek with a blue lightening streak down the starboard side. On the port side it had the name HOPE written in blue lettering. Mary Ann said, 'Hope . . . now that's a powerful word!' And she squeezed my hand real tight."

"What has that got to do with the fact that you think she cares for you?" Greg asked him again.

"Well, in the last letter I wrote to Mary Ann, nearly four weeks ago, I ended with this question, 'Mary Ann, is there any HOPE for the two of us?' Since she had not written me once the whole time I was in New York, I decided if she didn't answer I simply wouldn't write her again. Instead, I'd wait until I came home for Christmas and talk to her in person. Don't you see? This is my answer. There is HOPE for us! I wonder where she got this painting?" Morgan pondered.

"I think she must have painted it herself. I know she's been working diligently on something involving watercolors for the last few days. In fact, she's gotten very good at it. She told me she's been doing watercolors for about eight months," Greg said.

Soon they were pulling up in front of the Maxwell's house. The front door flew open as soon as Morgan stepped out of the carriage and out dashed Mary Ann right into his arms.

"Yes, Oh yes! There is HOPE for us. I've acted so ridiculous, Morgan, and I do apologize," Mary Ann said as she looked up into his eyes. "Did you like the way I told you that there is hope? I worked very hard to get the perfect likeness of our boat!"

"And it is a perfect likeness. You're quite talented, young lady. This picture will be placed on my desk so that I can see it every day," Morgan said as he drew her back into the circle of his arms.

"Let's go inside. Mother and father are anxious to see you also."

Phillip and Jane questioned Morgan about his newfound family. Their genuine interest and happiness for his mother, Elizabeth, as well as the rest of the family was evident as they listened with undivided attention to every word Morgan said. After all, Jane and Elizabeth had remained the best of friends all these years. Also, Jane Abigail Adams had accepted Phillip Gregory Maxwell's marriage proposal at Elizabeth's beloved Willow Place. It was the most beautiful place he could take Jane to propose, Phillip had told her. Phillip met Zachary through Elizabeth and they had become like brothers.

Morgan and Mary Ann excused themselves and left about four o'clock in the afternoon. Morgan told Mary Ann to bundle up because he had a special place he wanted to take her. It wasn't so very cold, but the wind always blew near the water. Morgan drove past the beach house into an area that was unfamiliar to Mary Ann. They went around a big curve and then the road took them almost straight up. The big Morgan horse took the hill in stride. They came to a plateau at the very top. Morgan pulled back on the reins saying, "Whoa, boy, whoa." He helped Mary Ann down from the carriage and they walked over near the edge of the plateau. They were standing high on a windy hill overlooking the beautiful James River. The sun was shining brightly, highlighting the lighter, brown streaks in Mary Ann's shoulder-length hair. Morgan thought he had never seen her look more beautiful. She looked as though she had stepped out of a dream.

Morgan held her close as she rested her head on his shoulder. He spoke softly and said, "Mary Ann, with all of my heart, I love you."

He tilted her chin and looked deep into her eyes and said, "Do I have permission to kiss you?" Not waiting for an answer he kissed her for the very first time.

Mary Ann caught her breath and Morgan saw a hint of a blush sweep over her face. She looked at him impishly, reached up and tousled his thick, black hair.

"And my heart belongs to you, Morgan. I've loved you since I was a little girl. Let me say I'm sorry I acted so immature about your going to New York. It had to be divine direction. Suppose you had not gone. Hannah and Elizabeth would never have found each other. Please forgive me, Morgan," she said, imploringly.

"You're forgiven, my love. Think no more about it."

They stood quietly, for ever so long, looking down on the river. They watched a steamboat go by. Two sailboats were moving gracefully as the wind caught their sails pushing them through the water with perfect ease. Some sea gulls were gliding high above the river. They had strayed from the ocean, which was not too far away. The sun was shining on the water making it sparkle like diamonds.

"Mary Ann, I discovered this beautiful, serene place quite some time ago. I've waited for just the right time to bring you here. I wanted the setting to be perfect when I asked you to be my wife." He gently turned her around so she was facing him, and continued, "Yes, I felt an urgency to go to New York, but when I saw how upsetting it was for you I almost scrapped the plan. However, there was still this urgency to go. While I've been up there I've kept busy, working very hard to learn all I can about shipping. But lately, I decided nothing is worth being away from you. I want you by my side for the journey ahead. Mary Ann, will you honor me by being my wife?"

"Morgan, my sweet Morgan, my heart has felt so empty since you've been away. Now, this very moment, my heart feels complete with the love we share. I'll be honored to be your wife. Granted, I'll not like being so far away from my parents. I love Williamsburg but I'm willing to go to New York with you. Since Mr. Bristol is your uncle, I know you have a golden opportunity to learn the trade of shipping by continuing to work there. Who knows what the Lord has planned for our lives. He just might have us live there for a period of time and then move us back to Williamsburg. Why, when you learn the business He just might have you buy back your grandfather Morgan's shipping company! I will unconditionally marry you and will feel safe having you to make those kinds of decisions for us." Having answered his question she reached up on tiptoe and gave him a kiss.

"Your nose is cold, Mary Ann! When I found this place and decided to save it for this special moment, I imagined it would be warm weather. We'll return this summer when we can spread a tablecloth and have a picnic."

"Is that a promise?"

"That's a promise!"

Chapter 25

Aunt Elizabeth, the guest room Amy and I are staying in is very tastefully decorated. It has a warm inviting charm to it. Where did you get the furniture for the room? Beth Lee asked.

"There's a story behind that room. When I went to Williamsburg to meet my grandparents, John and Catherine Morgan, for the first time, my room in their home contained that very same furniture. I remember how I felt when I entered the room. It was the most beautiful room I'd ever seen. The walls were off white with same colored draperies that were open over the large window allowing the sunlight to shimmer across the floor. Against the opposite wall stood that gorgeous white French provincial bed. The bedspread was made of heavy, white cotton and had a hand-embroidered candlewick design of tulips and ribbons with a six-inch border of crocheted lace fringe. The wash table, chest, and dressing table were matching French provincial. There were two white chairs covered in gold and silver patterns of brocade. A large picture of a romantic river scene, framed in white, was hanging over the bed," Elizabeth said.

"Why, Aunt Elizabeth, you've just described the guest room, exactly!"

"Yes, I know, my dear. You see, when Grandmother Catherine gave me that furniture, I stored it until we added the extra rooms on to Willow Place. Then I recreated the room just as it was in her beautiful home in Williamsburg. Savannah was tempted to make it her room after we finished it. But at that time she was all settled in upstairs and decided that we would make it into a guest room."

"I'm so glad that Amy and I have been able to 'enter into the past' by way of this room. Aunt Elizabeth, we're so happy to have you in our lives. We've discovered that we have a very strong family heritage. Because of the stories you've shared with us about our great grandparents, we feel as if we know them. Both the Baldwin's and the Morgan's were God-fearing examples to their children and grandchildren, and that heritage has been passed on to us, the great grandchildren.

"I might add that we absolutely adore Uncle Zachary. He held us all spellbound when he recounted his scary experience while sailing up the Chesapeake Bay. Morgan, Savannah, Amy and I are very blessed indeed that we have been raised to honor God in our lives and to know the power of prayer. Uncle Zachary and his brother, Ben, are no doubt here today because of answered prayer. Sometimes, because of the love of our heavenly Father and family, I feel as if I'm wrapped in a warm blanket and that I'm safe from all harm. Do you know what I mean, Aunt Elizabeth?" Beth Lee asked, wide-eyed."

"Yes indeed, I know exactly what you mean. You see, I was raised the very same way by my Grandmother Savannah and my 'Dandy.' They built a safe haven for me right here at Willow Place, my beautiful and beloved Willow Place. You, Beth

Lee, and Amy have stolen our hearts. We feel we've always had you in our lives. I can't tell you the feeling I have for Hannah. We're so much alike, not only in looks but in our values. Jordan, your father, is a prince of a man. There is absolutely no doubt that the Lord orchestrated our finding each other. It was His doing. His word tells us that 'a faithful man shall abound with blessings' and He has certainly bestowed His blessings on our family this Christmas season," Elizabeth proclaimed.

"Aunt Elizabeth, I have another question. Can you tell me more about Greg Maxwell's family? I understand from Greg that your family and his have been long-standing friends. How did you come to know them?"

"Jane and I became friends a couple of years before she was married. We were closer than friends. We felt we were kindred spirits. Phillip was also my friend. All three of us attended First Wesleyan. When Phillip and Zachary met they formed a lasting friendship. Our close association has remained constant over the years. We planned our vacations so we could spend quality time together."

"Where did you go and what did you do on your vacations?" Beth Lee inquired.

"Sometimes they would come to Willow Place. Horseback riding, camping and fishing were the order of the day much of the time. We would take turns at target practice. The boys became quite proficient in this sport. As they grew older, Morgan and Greg would often score higher than their fathers when the points were added up. Savannah and Mary Ann would climb trees and read books! We cooked our fish catch of the day over a campfire. Afterwards we'd sit around the fire and make up ghost stories. Lots of squealing and laughter erupted. We always said our bedtime prayers around the campfire. These were such meaningful times for all of us," Elizabeth said with a noticeable touch of nostalgia in her voice.

"I've grown quite fond of Greg since I've come to know him. The feeling seems to be mutual. He's no doubt very intelligent, a good conversationalist with an exceptional sense of humor, wouldn't you agree, Aunt Elizabeth?" Beth Lee asked.

"You have described him quite well, Beth Lee. He's all of that and more. He's gentle and tender and especially thoughtful of others. But then, you could say we are a little partial!" Elizabeth replied.

Savannah and Amy came into the sitting room rather noisily. They were laughing and talking like schoolgirls. They had ridden Thunder and Ginger out to the Baker Horse Farm for the afternoon.

"Mother, we're starved! We're going to hang up our coats and have some hot chocolate and applesauce cake. Do you and Beth Lee want to join us?" Savannah asked.

"That sounds good. Did you girls enjoy your ride? Your noses are red. It must be getting colder out," Elizabeth said. "We'll meet you in the breakfast room. I'll tell Rosie to prepare the refreshments."

"By the way, where are Dad, Uncle Jordan and Aunt Hannah?" Savannah inquired as she turned to leave the room.

"Your dad took them on a tour of the carriage factory. They should be home any minute."

"Beth Lee, you should've gone with us. Vann and Clint asked where you were. There's a very handsome cowboy named Hank who works for the Baker's. You should meet him!" Amy exclaimed.

"I'll leave the cowboys to you and Savannah. Besides, Aunt Elizabeth and I have enjoyed our time together this afternoon," Beth Lee replied.

"Indeed we have," Elizabeth said, as she shooed the girls out the door. Turning to Beth Lee she said, "Let's go get that hot chocolate brewing."

Chapter 26

Sitting around the open fire in the library after the evening meal, Elizabeth asked, "Jordan, what do you think of the carriage operation and the plant?"

"It's a fascinating business, much more detailed than I ever imagined. No wonder Zachary's been so successful in its operation. It's evident the workers are producing a quality carriage that's equal to and surpasses some of the carriages produced in New York," Jordan said positively.

"I was particularly impressed with the way the seats are made. The springs, padding and quality of the seat coverings help determine the comfort to a great degree, Zachary pointed out to us," Hannah offered.

"Speaking of businesses, how difficult was the transition from overseeing a large plantation to managing a shipping business for your father-in-law, Jordan? Those are two vastly different occupations," Zachary remarked. "Did he ever discuss this with you?"

"Yes, on many occasions. Mr. Anderson enjoyed reminiscing about 'those days' as he called them. He said the change was so vastly different that he was reminded quite often of something Abraham Lincoln once said, and he would quote . . . 'I have been driven to my knees many times because there was no place else to go.' He said that he and the Lord got to be very good friends during his tenure of learning the shipping business! At times, when he thought he might have made a mistake, a great Shakespearean quote would come to mind . . . 'Doubt is a thief that often makes us fear to tread where we might have won.' These two sayings helped to keep him on track. Also, there was an 'old salt' who was working for the company when he bought it. He learned quickly and a lot from this dear old sailor named Thomas. He also inherited a couple of men in the deal who had worked in the office for years. They were invaluable employees. The dock crew was like no other, I remember him saying. He told me he felt he was born to do that kind of work. I highly respected Mr. Anderson. He took me under his wing and taught me the shipping business. I, too, have loved shipping. It was working for Mr. Anderson that I met and won the love of his daughter, Hannah. What a bonus this has been!" Jordan said as he smiled at his wife.

"From what you've told me, you had a very good relationship with Hannah's father," Zachary said thoughtfully.

"Besides my own father, Mr. Anderson became my mentor, and Mrs. Anderson was like a second mother to me," Jordan replied. "They never made a difference between me and Hannah."

"I'm so glad you had such a loving couple to take you as their own, Hannah. The Lord was looking after you from the beginning," Elizabeth said.

"Indeed He was and still is, especially blessing me with a husband like Jordan."

"That reminds me, Elizabeth, we haven't really discussed the incident that happened some 18 years ago during the war when I and some of my men stormed Willow Place for food and water. I'm so very sorry for the fright we caused you and the children. When I saw you it was as if Hannah was standing before me with our two children. I was stunned at the resemblance. I felt that I needed to hug you and comfort you rather than make demands of you. That scene haunted me throughout the rest of the war and I've really never forgotten it. I beg your forgiveness. But I'll have to say, I so admired your spirit and calmness during such a harrowing experience," Jordan said.

"It was very frightening. But I knew you were a gentleman when you stopped the men with you from making advances with me. And I well remember your saying that this war would do more harm to the North and South than good. You came and left quickly. I was so thankful for that. We met, then, in very trying circumstances. We have met again under such wonderful circumstances. The Lord works in mysterious ways His wonders to perform, wouldn't you agree?" Elizabeth said to all of them.

"By the way, Jordan, what happened after I captured you and two of your men trying to swim to the Galena to escape that very same night? I've meant to ask you several times since you've been here but other things crowded out that question," Zachary inquired.

This led to an exciting and long recounting of Jordan's tenure in the Confederate army during the Civil War years.

Chapter 27

*M*organ, Mary Ann and Greg came from Williamsburg on December 31st to spend New Year's Eve with Morgan's family, and also to tell the family the good news that Morgan and Mary Ann were engaged. Elizabeth became teary-eyed when she heard the news. Nothing could make her and Zachary happier. Savannah was ecstatic that she would finally have a "sister."

The Baker's invited all of them to a New Year's Eve and birthday dinner party. After ringing in the New Year at midnight, they all wished Vann a happy 25th birthday. His parents and Clint gave him a new saddle and saddle blanket. He opened token gifts from the others. While they were saying their goodbyes Savannah called Vann aside so she could give him her gift. They were standing outside on the front porch in the reflection of the gaslights. Savannah handed him a nicely wrapped box she had left in a chair on the porch earlier. He gave a low whistle and said, "This box is considerably heavier than the one I gave you on your birthday! I can't imagine . . ."

"Hurry and open it!" Savannah said excitedly.

"You didn't! But you did!" Vann exclaimed. "You got me the spurs I've been admiring for so long. I really need them, too. What with my new saddle, blanket and now these, I'm all set for another year's work around here. How did you know I wanted these spurs?"

"Remember, I was with you a few weeks ago when you went to the feed store. You picked up these spurs and turned them over in your hand and commented how much you liked them. I knew then they were the perfect gift for your upcoming birthday."

"I must say this is the happiest birthday I've ever had. Savannah, how could I be so lucky as to have you in my life? Your love and the wonderful meaning it's brought to me is a priceless gift, one I shall always treasure."

With that, he held her very close in the cold night air and whispered, "Savannah, my little Savannah, how I do love you." He leaned down and kissed her lips, not once but twice.

January 1, 1881 was the last day of the Bristol's visit. They would be going back to New York along with Morgan and Greg on the second. They decided to spend the day together, reliving the past two weeks.

Morgan and Mary Ann had not set a date for their wedding. Parting for them was very hard. Being separated was not going to be easy, but they had to make the right choices for their future and that would take some time and planning.

The Bristol's goodbyes were sad, yet exciting, as they made plans for future visits and staying in close touch with one another. They waved and shouted goodbye as the big iron machine huffed and puffed, leaving the Richmond Train Depot heading for New York.

Sitting around the roaring fire on the sofa that same evening, Elizabeth and Zachary were reflecting over the time they spent with Hannah, Jordan and the girls. It had been a glorious visit. It still seemed unreal, but it had added depth and strength to their family unit.

"The Lord has blessed us abundantly, Elizabeth. We've had some hard times but most of our years have been good ones. He's promised us the abundant life if we put our faith and trust in Him. We were blessed to be taught His word growing up. Then holding these truths dear, we've taught them to our children. I'd say, Elizabeth, it's a wonderful life. Yes indeed, a very wonderful life!" Zachary said.

"I suppose our minds run together. I was thinking those same thoughts. I remember David wrote in Psalms . . .' But the mercy of the Lord is from everlasting to everlasting upon them that fear him and his righteousness unto children's children; To such as keep his covenant, and to those that remember his commandments to do them.' The entire 103rd Psalm is a wonderful description of God's bountiful mercy. I agree with you that we've had a good life," Savannah replied.

"Well, Elizabeth dear, we are in the second day of 1881. This year will be our 25th Wedding Anniversary! I suggest we do something extra special to celebrate come November 16th. Got any ideas?" Zachary said, as he pulled Elizabeth closer to him.

Laying her head on his shoulder she replied, "I'm surprised you thought of our anniversary with all that's been going on. Yes, I've got some ideas. I've thought of a lot of things. But this is an event we need to plan together. Morgan and Savannah are grown now and have interests of their own. I think we need to devote more time to each other. You're my very heart-beat, Zachary. My love for you is ever bit as exciting now as it was the first day we were married. When you walk into a room of people you fill the whole space and I see no one but you. My love for you knows no bounds and has no limits. Our twenty-four years together, Zachary, have never been a disappoint-ment, but always, always fulfilling. Oh, how much I love you!" Elizabeth declared passionately.

"You've always had a way with words, Princess. I want you to know what you say fills my heart with appreciation and gratitude. I remember how overwhelmed I was the first time I saw you at the train depot. You've never lost that charm. Do you suppose I could have a kiss?" Zachary said as he stood and pulled her to her feet so he could hold her close.

Chapter 28

MONDAY, MARCH 10, 1881

The sun had burned off the early morning fog and it was a glorious day. Yesterday's rain had washed everything clean and the bright sunshine was dancing on the waters of the lake. The willow trees were swaying in the March wind. Savannah felt it was a good day to be alive. She and her mother were sitting on the front porch having a late cup of coffee. They were discussing wedding plans for Savannah and Vann.

"Mother, after talking with Vann's mother yesterday we settled on Saturday, May 17th as the date for the wedding. They agreed with you that the 17th rather than the 10th would probably give us more favorable weather for a lakeside wedding. I want to thank you, Mother, and also Dad, for permitting me to have the wedding of my dreams. You've both been wonderful about it all."

"Well, Savannah, your dad and I chose not to have a big wedding. We loved the planning of our secret elopement. It was very romantic. However, Grandmother Catherine and Grandfather Morgan would have given me a grand wedding had I wanted one. Your father and I are happy that you want to be married here at Willow Place. It will endear this place to us even more. With the proper planning we can make it everything you want it to be. So let's begin to do some planning now."

"I've made some sketches for the reception and the altar area. Please look at them, Mother, and see what you think. We'll need to decide on flowers and color choices. Actually, I'm getting a little ahead of myself. I have a list here and we need to take things one at a time," Savannah said, as she opened a tablet of notes.

They decided they could accommodate 60 people comfortably, including the wedding party. With that settled, wedding invitations must be selected, ordered and prepared for mailing in plenty of time. Elizabeth suggested they use flowers from the gardens around Willow Place for centerpieces for the fifteen guest tables. Hopefully they would have roses from their rose garden by then.

"Savannah, suppose we look for your wedding dress on Saturday. If we can't find what you like we might have to order it. We could also select your invitations," Elizabeth suggested. "After all, it's only two months until the wedding."

Abney's Department Store had recently enlarged its bridal section. Long-time friend Mary Ella Abney warmly greeted Elizabeth and Savannah as they entered the store.

They exchanged pleasantries and then Mary Ella seated them to look over the new selection of wedding invitations. It didn't take Savannah long to choose her favorite. She liked the traditional engraved invitation in script.

Next, they entered the room where the formal wedding gowns were on display. Savannah caught her breath in awe.

She was so overwhelmed by the beauty she stopped and stared. Mary Ella and Elizabeth looked at each other, smiling, and said nothing. Finally, Savannah walked directly to a particular gown displayed in an area by itself, stopped and said, "They're all very beautiful, but this one is elegant! Mother, don't you agree? Isn't it the most gorgeous dress you've ever seen?"

Mary Ella said, "We've only had this dress a few days. It's a Queen Victoria from Worth of Paris. Notice the quality of the ecru satin. It's trimmed with delicate Honiton lace. The half-capped sleeve with the off-shoulder neckline will look especially nice on you, Savannah. Don't you agree, Elizabeth?" Mary Ella asked as she turned to see Elizabeth's reaction.

"It's very beautiful. Savannah, why don't you try it on? We can tell more about it then," Elizabeth said.

There was no doubt this was the dress for Savannah. It fit her perfectly and would require no alterations. Yards of fabric at the back of the skirt were gathered up forming a bustle. A court train was attached at the waist just underneath the bustle.

As Savannah walked the length of the room and back several times, she looked like a dream walking. Elizabeth felt tears well up in her eyes. Could this be her little girl that loved riding horses, grooming them personally and even cleaning out their stalls . . . this vision of loveliness? She realized at this moment that Savannah was embarking on a different journey in life. She would be leaving their home and making one of her own.

A feeling of emptiness swept over her, momentarily, but was lifted as she heard Savannah's voice.

"Mother, may I have this dress? Please! It's everything I've dreamed of for my wedding day."

"I can tell by the expression on your face and the lilt in your voice that we need to look no further, my child. Of course you may have it," Elizabeth said, looking with adoration at her daughter.

Chapter 29

The Lee Dyer family that bought John and Catherine Morgan's house on the hill above the lake at Willow Place had decided to move to Georgia. When they bought the house it was agreed that if they ever decided to sell, it would go back to Zachary and Elizabeth. The Dyers moved the last week of March. The house was left in mint condition. Zachary did have the inside painted which gave it a fresh look.

After an early supper on Friday, Zachary and Elizabeth were sitting on a bench near the lake watching the ducks.

"I've been thinking about Grandfather Morgan's house, Zachary. It's empty now and I don't like the idea of selling it to anyone, especially strangers. I have an idea I want to share with you and see what you think about it."

"Before you tell me, I'm sure what you have in mind is what I've been thinking about. Does it have to do with Savannah and Vann?" Zachary asked.

"Yes, it does. It's six weeks until their wedding. They'll have to have a place to live, or I should say they will want a place of their own. I know how much Savannah loves Willow Place, and she loves her grandfather and grandmother's house. I think we should make it a wedding present to Savannah and Vann. What do you think?"

"I agree with you. However, I'm not too sure how Vann will react to such a gift. He's a very independent young man," Zachary said reflectively.

"Let's tell Savannah that we wish to talk to them this weekend. We'll see what their reaction is. It would solve the problem of the house for us. I don't want to let it stand empty again," Elizabeth said.

After seating themselves at the breakfast table Saturday morning, Savannah asked, "Mother, have you noticed how the flowers have started to bloom in the gardens? Today is April 5th. By the week of the wedding they should be beautiful, don't you agree?"

"Yes, thanks to the special care Bill and Leo are giving the plants, we should have an abundant supply for the wedding," her mother replied.

"Savannah, your mother and I would like to talk with you and Vann. Does he plan to come by tonight?"

"As a matter of fact he plans to come this afternoon. But what do you want to talk to us about?" Savannah asked.

"You'll see when he gets here, my child."

In the early afternoon Savannah, Vann, Elizabeth and Zachary were walking down near the boat dock at the south end of the lake. The grounds around Willow Place had never looked lovelier. They had been talking excitedly about the wedding plans, where exactly to place the chairs, the best spot to have the altar and tables for the reception luncheon. These plans had been changed several times. But it had all been lots of fun.

They were laughing, saying they just might forget which plan they had settled on by the time preparations had to be made for the wedding.

Elizabeth remarked, "I've heard it said that anticipation is greater than reality. We've found that anticipation for this wedding has been great. Soon we'll see how reality measures up!"

"Another suggestion, if I may," Zachary said. "Why not have a white gazebo built at the north end of the lake for the ceremony and have the luncheon at the south end of the lake? Here the serpentine garden path would add a lot of charm to the luncheon. What do you think?"

"Perfect, absolutely perfect. This idea is the best one yet!" Savannah exclaimed. "Is this what you wanted to talk to me and Vann about?"

"No. I'll let your mother tell you what we have in mind."

"Your father and I want to give you and Vann a special wedding present. It will mean a great deal to us if you'll accept it. You are aware that the Dyer's have sold Grandfather Morgan's house back to us and that it now stands empty. We don't want to resell it. It would be doing us a favor if you two would accept it as a wedding present."

"Whoa, wait just a minute! What you are proposing is very generous indeed. Please don't think me ungrateful but I can't accept such a gift as this. Savannah will be my responsibility. It will be my place to provide for her," Vann said emphatically.

"Vann, we understand how you feel, but think about it before you refuse our offer. Willow Place is the only home Savannah has ever known. She grew up here and has some good memories of her Morgan grandparents and their home. She's said repeatedly that she never wants to leave Willow Place.

You and your family came here some five years ago, built a home, established a horse farm and, according to Savannah, you're very fond of this area. It's reasonable for you two to accept the Morgan house as your very own. You can't imagine how it would relieve our minds to have you accept it as our gift to you," Zachary said.

"Vann, please say yes. I love this place. We both would be close to our parents. It's also close to your work. If we had children we would want to do the same for them if we could. You've said before how much you like the house and its surroundings. Please, Vann, please?" Savannah lamented.

"You all have caught me by surprise. I'll have to think about it," Vann replied.

"May I ask where you two plan to live after you're married?" Elizabeth asked.

"We've looked at two houses for rent on this side of Richmond. We're trying to decide which one we like best. This will be only until we can build," Vann answered.

"We don't wish to interfere in your plans but you're our children. It's our great pleasure to do good things for you. This will be a gift with no strings attached. It will be deeded to you to do with as you please," Elizabeth said. "We'll await your answer, Vann."

"Savannah and I will discuss it further and let you know soon what our decision is. Your generosity overwhelms me."

Chapter 30

Vann and Savannah were riding over Willow Place Sunday afternoon. They rode around the lake and up the hill to the Morgan house. Sitting atop their mounts, they looked out over the grand view of the valley beneath them on one side and the mountain range on the other. This was indeed a spectacular view, quite calming and peaceful.

Vann looked at Savannah and saw a tear falling down her cheek.

"What's wrong? Why are you crying?" Vann asked.

"I think I'm just overwhelmed by the beauty of this place. The things I hold most dear can be seen from this vantage point. God's creation of the universe is revealed in this small corner of the world in a majestic way, just as far as the eye can see. Willow Place is a part of my heart."

Vann dismounted and tethered his horse. He reached up for Savannah and lifted her down from her horse straight into his arms. He held her close and swayed gently to and fro.

"Savannah, my adorable Savannah. You sound almost homesick and we haven't even said our vows yet! Your happiness is of primary importance to me. You really do want us to accept your parents wedding gift of this house, don't you?"

"Yes, Vann, I do. If we build a house, where will we build it?" she asked.

"Father is going to give me some acreage on our place to build on."

"What is the difference in your father giving us land and my parents giving us a house?"

"The difference is I'll pay my father back for the land. I'll tell you what we'll do. We can move into the Morgan house but we'll pay your parents for it. What they do with the money is up to them. If they want to put it in a trust for you then that will be fine. We'll negotiate a price. If they wish to mark some off as a wedding present then we'll accept that. Will this make you happy, dear Savannah?"

"Yes, oh yes! And I think this arrangement will be fair," Savannah said as she gave him a grateful smile. "Could we go now and tell them our decision?"

"Sure, but first let's sit on the porch steps and talk a little while."

Savannah was a picture of loveliness. The blue long-sleeved blouse she was wearing was the same shade blue as her eyes. Her denim riding skirt stopped at her ankles, exposing her brown, leather riding boots. She was wearing her blonde hair in an upsweep. Curly strands framed her face. When she smiled at Vann her dimples were so charming he could hardly deny her anything.

"Savannah, I hope you won't think I'm being ungrateful about the house situation. You see, I've been taught to work for what I get. My parents have been good to Clint and me. But hard work has been drilled into me. My father has two favorite sayings he quotes often. The first one is from Thomas Edison. 'Opportunity is missed by most people because it is dressed in overalls and looks like work.' The second one is from Theodore Roosevelt. He said, 'Far and away the best prize that life offers is the chance to work hard at work worth doing.' Since becoming a man I appreciate this philosophy. We seem to appreciate what we obtain more if we work for it. I firmly believe this, Savannah."

"I admire you, Vann, for your high standard. I would never want you to change. I'll admit your dashing good looks first attracted me to you. Your riding skills thrilled me as I watched you riding past Willow Place when you and your family first moved to this area. But as I have gotten to know you personally, I like what I see in your inner man best of all. These qualities make for a firm foundation in a family unit. Knowing your sterling qualities, I'd love you even if you were that squatty, bow-legged, crooked-nosed fellow that Morgan described you as being!" Savannah said with feigned seriousness.

"What? When did he say that? And you mean you *let* him talk about me like that?" Vann said sputtering and pretending outrage.

"Calm down, Vann. No, I set him straight quickly."

"I'm vindicated then with nothing to worry about. So let's go speak with your parents about our decision concerning the Morgan house, soon to be the Baker's house!"

Chapter 31

Saturday, May 17, 1881

The rain poured, the thunder rolled and the lightening flashed. "No! No! Surely not rain on my wedding day. It just can't be raining after all the plans we've made to have the wedding outside." Savannah was wound up in the bed covers and felt her breath was being cut off. "This can't be happening!" she sobbed.

"Mother! Mother! You must stop the rain. You can't let it rain on my wedding day. Where's father? Tell him to make it stop!"

"Savannah, Savannah, wake up. You are having a bad dream. Wake up, dear," Elizabeth said as she shook Savannah gently.

"There, there, my little girl. Do you think for one minute I'd permit it to rain on your wedding day?" her father said as he stroked her forehead and rocked her to and fro in his strong arms.

"Was I really dreaming, Father? You mean it really isn't raining? But it sounded so real. I even heard the thunder and saw the flash of lightening."

"Believe me, it isn't raining. The sky outside is full of stars and a full moon is shining very brightly. You've worried it might rain so much these last few days that you dreamed you heard rain. That's all, my sweet little girl. Go back to sleep now. You want to look your best tomorrow," Zachary said as he tucked her in and gave her a kiss on the forehead.

The morning of May 17th could not have been more perfect. Willow Place was a witness to God's creation of beauty. The blooming shrubs and a variety of May flowers exploded in color as the weeping willow trees bowed gracefully to the splendor all around them. Spring flowers decorated the gazebo and white chairs were arranged perfectly for the wedding guests.

Pastel cuttings from the ground gardens were arranged beautifully and placed as centerpieces on the tables for the reception meal. Elizabeth and Savannah used family china, crystal, and silver from the Baldwin's and the Morgan's, along with Elizabeth's collection, making her reception even more special. They had the food catered in which was a relief to Elizabeth.

The wedding cake was made by Durden's Bakery. It was a three-tiered cake topped with real pink roses. Savannah thought it was the most beautiful cake she'd ever seen.

Jordan and Hannah Bristol, Beth Lee and Amy had come a week before the wedding. Beth Lee was Savannah's maid of honor. Amy was a bridesmaid along with Mary Ann Maxwell.

Vann's brother, Clint, was best man. Morgan and Hank Stephenson were groomsmen.

Arriving guests were completely taken aback by the beauty they beheld.

The stringed musicians began to play and a hush fell over those in attendance. The bridesmaids were lovely in their pastel dresses of pink, yellow and green.

When Savannah walked down the rose petal strewn pathway to the altar at the gazebo, escorted by her father, Elizabeth could not help but wipe away a tear. Savannah was radiant in her Queen Victoria wedding gown. Vann, so handsome in his cutaway morning coat and ascot tie, smiled broadly as he watched his bride approach the altar where he was waiting.

Pastor David Autry did the traditional wedding ceremony in such an eloquent manner. It was very meaningful to the bride and groom. He spoke to them personally, giving them some sage advice as they embarked on this journey of life.

After all the festivities of the day ended and the new Mr. and Mrs. Vann Baker were preparing to leave, a brand new white carriage drawn by a handsome white horse was awaiting them. The carriage had pink satin streamers and roses attached to the back along with a sign reading JUST MARRIED.

The excited and happy couple had arranged to change clothes at the Richmond Hotel where their luggage was waiting. They left on the afternoon train for their honeymoon to Savannah, Georgia.

Chapter 32

MONDAY, SEPTEMBER 8, 1881

Fred Stone sat at a table in his dimly lit room in the rundown hotel on the lower, south side of Richmond. He had unfolded the newspaper article about the wedding of Savannah Bainbridge and Vann Brown in May of this year. He had read it so many times it was getting worn. His money from the bank he had robbed in Lynchburg six months ago was running out. He was going to have to put his plan into action.

Fred had come to Richmond the last of March from Lynchburg. He had never robbed a bank before but had been successful on his first try. He had hidden inside the bank at Lynchburg and waited until after it closed. The combination to the bank's safe was not hard to find. He opened it, stuffed his pockets full of money and escaped into the dark of night.

This Bainbridge family was bound to have lots of money. He knew that Zachary Bainbridge owned the Bainbridge Carriage Company. The big wedding he gave his daughter proved they were not hurting for money. Since the wedding in May he had found out all he could about this family. He knew where they lived. He knew that Mrs. Bainbridge did volunteer work at West Richmond Hospital. Dr. David Blake was the surgeon general there. Fred had snooped around the hospital and picked up a white doctor's coat. He felt very confident about his plan. It would work. It had to! He would implement it day after tomorrow on September 10th.

Finally daylight came. Fred had not slept very well. He had begun to think seriously about what he was planning to do. Did he really want to do this? He knew kidnapping was a serious offense. What would his dear mother think if she found out? He knew his father would be disappointed that he had raised a son who would do such a thing. Robbing his home-town bank was bad enough. How did he ever get into such a mess? Worst of all, he could hear a still small voice saying . . . "What shall it profit a man if he should gain the whole world and lose his own soul?"

With daylight he was able to push the fears and questions into the background. He knew he needed money. This seemed to be a way to get it quickly. Besides, he had no intentions of harming Mrs. Bainbridge. He cleaned himself up, had break-fast and then waited for early afternoon to arrive.

Fred went to Luke's Livery Stable, rented a carriage and hooked his horse to it. He then made his way to the Bainbridge house. He was wearing the white doctor's coat. Seeing some-one sitting on a bench near the large lake, he checked the reins and stopped the carriage. He stepped down and walked quickly toward the bench. Elizabeth stood to her feet. She recognized the doctor's coat but not the person who was wear-ing it.

"Are you Mrs. Bainbridge?" Fred asked urgently.

"Why yes. Yes, I am," Elizabeth answered.

"Dr. Blake has sent me for you. Your husband has been badly injured at the carriage plant. He said you were to come at once."

"But who are you? What happened to Zachary? How was he injured?"

"I'm Joseph Landers, the new assistant in the emergency area of the hospital. I saw you last week when you were doing volunteer work. Don't you remember?"

"No, I can't say that I do. I need to get Albert to take me and let someone know what has happened," Elizabeth said, sort of in a daze.

"I don't think you understand, Mrs. Bainbridge. We must go now or it could be too late. Your husband was badly injured."

Elizabeth let him guide her to the carriage and quickly help her inside. He turned the carriage around and left, urging the horse to go faster.

Elizabeth's only thought was of Zachary. How could he have been injured? How long ago did it happen? This nice young man was certainly hurrying as fast as the horse would go. She tried to recall if she had seen him at the hospital but she simply could not remember him. She closed her eyes, leaned forward in the carriage and began to pray.

"Lord, our strength and protector, I ask you to be with my Zachary. I don't know what his injuries are, but Lord you do. Give the doctors wisdom as they tend to his needs. Please don't let these injuries end his life. He's too young, Lord, and I need him so. I ask for mercy now, Lord, for Zachary and for me," ending her prayer with a sob.

The carriage stopped and the young man was beside her before Elizabeth got her bearings from having her eyes closed in prayer. He pulled a cloth from his white coat pocket and placed it over her mouth and nose, holding it tightly. She breathed deeply, felt light-headed, struggled in vain and then became unconscious.

Fred laid her down in the seat of the carriage so she couldn't be seen. He drove to the room of the hotel where he was staying. His room was just inside the door on the left. He slipped inside to see if he could see anyone. The attendant at the front desk was slumped over in a dead sleep and there was no one else in sight. He quickly picked Elizabeth up and whisked her into his room. He put her on the bed and tied her hands over her head to the bedpost. He stuffed her mouth with a cloth, loosely so she wouldn't suffocate, and tied a folded bandanna around her mouth to hold the cloth in place. Then he tied her feet together. She was still fast asleep.

He must hurry before she awakened. He locked the door and left in the carriage. He took the carriage back to the livery stable. He had written a note to Zachary that read:

> If you want to see your wife alive again you will put $10,000.00 in a paper bag and leave it under the large oak tree on the left side of the road at the south end of town. There is a large rock under the tree. Place the money under the rock. You have until Thursday evening at 6:00. If the money is not there you will have a hard time finding the remains of your wife, Elizabeth. If you contact the police I will know it and I won't even wait for the money. You will never see Elizabeth again.

Fred quickly went to the carriage company. He knew exactly where Zachary's carriage was parked. He looked in all directions and could see no one. Laying the note in the carriage on the front seat, he ran back to his horse and quickly left.

Returning to the hotel room, he found Elizabeth still asleep. He hoped he didn't give her too much chloroform. He raised one of her eyelids to peer at her pupil. She stirred a little indicating she was all right. He removed the cloth from her mouth and just let her sleep. About eight o'clock she began to put up a struggle. He noticed that she began to heave. He untied her arms. The chloroform had made her very sick. She threw up a couple of times. He wet a cloth from the water pitcher on the table and sponged her face and neck. She slumped back against the pillow. All the color had drained from her face. She looked helpless and pitiful but was also very beautiful.

"If you'll be quiet and still, I won't shackle you to the bed again. But one wrong move and you'll be gagged and tied up. Do you understand?"

"Yes. I understand," Elizabeth answered in a very weak voice. "But why are you doing this? Is my husband okay?"

"Indeed he's all right. I'm doing this for money. You see, I need money. That's something you wouldn't understand, fair lady. But if your husband wants to ever see you again he'll give me the money I've asked for and I'll be on my way."

"So you've kidnapped me for money. You're a fine looking young man, I'd say about 25, and you're resorting to this kind of action for money? How sad. How very sad, and what a waste."

"That's enough. I don't need a lecture. Say no more."

FIVE P.M. AT THE CARRIAGE PLANT . . .

Zachary walked slowly toward his carriage, breathing in the autumn-like cool air. He always loved the fall of the year. Harvest time . . . the time of reaping of one's labor after the planting season. Yes, he felt it was good to be alive. He went inside Luke's Livery Stable, fetched Maude and hooked her up to his carriage that was parked in his special place at the plant. The ride home this afternoon was going to be a pleasure!

He opened the carriage door and saw something white lying on the front seat. It was a neatly written note. As he read it he couldn't believe his eyes! He felt as if he'd been hit in the stomach.

"Elizabeth, Elizabeth, my love, what's he done to you? Where are you? I must find you quickly!" Zachary said aloud, even though no one was there to hear.

He knew he must contact the police in spite of what the note said. Time was of the essence. This maniac could be torturing Elizabeth at this very moment.

He drove directly to the police station, jumped out of the carriage and ran inside, waving the single page note in the air. He went straight into the Police Inspector's office unannounced.

"Inspector Richardson, I need help now!" and he put the letter on his desk.

Inspector Richardson quickly read the letter, then stood to his feet and said, "Zachary, where did this letter come from? How did you get it? What time did you receive it? When did you last see Elizabeth?"

Zachary gave the inspector all the information he asked for. They both looked over the letter again, carefully.

"Zachary, this letter is well written. You will notice the spelling is correct. He's an educated man. The paper the letter is written on is quality paper. It's not soiled. I'd say the man is not likely to do harm to Elizabeth. He needs money or wants money the easy way, without working for it. Let me get some officers in here to begin a search and to ask some questions around town. You go on home now and get in touch with Vann and Savannah. Send Albert, your overseer, into town. He can help us with this. You all stay there in case Elizabeth comes home or you receive another message. Let us take care of this."

"But inspector, this man is asking for money and he gives us a dead line! I'll gladly give him the money. My only concern is to get Elizabeth back quickly and unharmed. I'm not too sure your way is the right way to go. I can get in touch with my banker now, get the money, and take it to the place this man spoke of. I think I know the very tree he's talking about. After all, what is money without Elizabeth? What is my life without Elizabeth?" Zachary lamented.

"Zachary, listen to me. We are trained to handle these kinds of situations. Let us do our job. You also need to send a telegram to Morgan about his mother. He needs to know. Go now so we can get started."

"Yes, I must let Morgan and the Bristol's know as well as Savannah and Vann. But I'll be back. If you can't find Elizabeth or her kidnapper, then we must do as he has asked and give him the money by his deadline. I cannot . . . I will not take a chance with Elizabeth's life."

Zachary sent Morgan a telegram telling him about his mother and advising him to come home at once. Then he headed for Willow Place as fast as Maude could go. He went straight to the stable and told Albert what had happened and sent him to see Inspector Richardson.

He entered the house through the back door calling out to Rosie. She was in the kitchen preparing supper.

"Rosie, when did you see Elizabeth last?"

"She went out to sit by the lake and read about 2:00 this afternoon. I went to look for her at 3:30 but she wasn't there. She often walks up the hill to Miss Savannah's in the afternoon. I suppose she's still up there."

"No, Rosie, she isn't. I only wish she were. Rosie, I've some bad news for you. Elizabeth has been kidnapped."

An incredulous expression swept over Rosie's face, a look of total disbelief.

"Sir, what are you talking about?"

"Elizabeth has been kidnapped from her own front lawn. I have a note asking for ransom money. Did you see anyone around here this afternoon at any time, Rosie? Did you hear anything, a carriage maybe, or the sound of horses' hooves?"

"No sir, Mr. Zachary. I didn't see anyone nor hear anything. Oh, Mr. Zachary, what are you going to do?" Rosie said as she slumped in a chair at the table.

"I must go and tell Savannah and ask her and Vann to come here right away. We'll be right back," he said as he ran out the door and up the hill to the 'Morgan' house.

Zachary banged on the front door and then threw it open calling out, "Savannah, Vann, where are you?"

Vann appeared in the sitting room door from the kitchen area saying, "Here we are Mr. Bainbridge. Come on in, we're in the kitchen." Looking at Zachary's colorless face Vann asked, "What in the world is wrong?"

"Savannah, Vann, my children, I have some terrible news. I don't know how to tell you except to say that Elizabeth has been kidnapped and a ransom has been demanded."

"Father, what are you saying? What do you mean mother has been kidnapped? How do you know? She's been here at home. I saw her sitting by the lake this afternoon. Have you been to the house to see if she's there?"

"Savannah, listen to me my dear child. When I went to my carriage after leaving the plant for the day, there was a ransom note on the front seat of the carriage. The kidnapper is asking for a $10,000.00 ransom."

"Oh, Father, what are we going to do? Vann, you can find her. I know you can. You can do anything," Savannah pleaded as she went from her father to her husband.

Vann felt so helpless but he held her close and told her, "We'll find her, Savannah. You'll see, we'll find her just like we found you when you were lost."

Zachary said, "We must go down to the house in case we receive another note or, by some miracle, your mother might return."

The three of them held hands as they walked down the hill. They hurried up the front steps, down the hallway and into the kitchen. There they gathered around the kitchen table. Rosie poured them some hot apple cider because she didn't know what else to do. She felt the need to be busy.

"Savannah, you said you saw your mother sitting by the lake this afternoon. What time was it?" Zachary asked.

It was 3:30 when I came out on the front porch and waved to her. I thought she would walk up to the house and was surprised when she didn't. She was reading so I went back inside still thinking she would come up a little later. But she never did. I came back out on the porch at 4:00 and she was no longer on the bench. Rosie, did she come back inside?

"No, she didn't. I thought she was at your house until your father came in and told me what had happened," Rosie said tearfully.

"Mr. Bainbridge, I'm going into town and see what Inspector Richardson and his men are doing and see what I can do to help, that is, with your permission."

"Vann, I think that's a good idea. I'd like to go but Inspector Richardson asked that I stay here. Please stay in touch and let us know what's going on. We'll be so anxious. And Vann, you're a real son to us. Always know this."

"Savannah, I'll count on you to be strong," Vann said as he held her close and kissed her goodbye.

As he was preparing to leave they heard a knock on the door. Rosie ushered Pastor David Autry and his wife, Emily, into the kitchen. Savannah ran into the arms of Emily and let the older woman sooth her tears away with a mother's touch. Zachary felt much better to have their support at a time like this.

Chapter 33

Manhattan, New York

A little before six o'clock in the evening Morgan heard
a knock on his door. It was a messenger from the telegraph
office. Signing for the telegram, he hurriedly ripped it open.
In it was the dreadful message that his beloved mother had
been kidnapped. He was stunned. Quickly stuffing the telegram into his coat pocket, he ran downstairs to the street and
hailed a carriage. He must go tell the Bristol's and make plans
to catch the early morning train to Richmond.

The Bristol's were shocked at the alarming news Morgan
brought to them. Greg Maxwell had a dinner date with Beth
Lee and was present when Morgan arrived. They all rallied
around Morgan, trying to console him.

"This just can't be happening," Hannah said, "not when
Elizabeth and I have just found each other! How dreadful!
Elizabeth must be frightened half to death."

"We're so far away it makes us feel completely helpless. In times like these you want to be doing something . . . to lend a hand! There are so many questions we want to ask," Jordan said, "so much we could be doing if we were only there."

"I'll catch the first train out in the morning," Morgan said. But since we can't be there we can pray to One who is there, One who knows exactly where mother is and can send angels to help her. One of mother's favorite scriptures, one that I've heard her quote so many times, says . . . 'The angel of the Lord encampeth round about them that fear him, and delivereth them.' In her hour of need I'm certain she's said this scripture over and over in her mind. "I have to believe that the Lord will protect my mother, else I couldn't stand it," Morgan said with an emotionally stressed voice. "Uncle Jordan, would you pray for my mother?"

As Jordan prayed for Elizabeth, a blessed peace settled over the family. God's presence brought a calming spirit to each of them.

It was 10:00 P.M. Fred Stone had some bread and fruit in his hotel room. He offered Elizabeth a sampling and she chose an orange. She was very thirsty and still a bit nauseous. Bowing her head, Elizabeth asked the Lord's blessings on the morsel. Then peeling the orange, she ate the sections slowly. It was very sweet and tasty. It helped to settle her stomach and gave her some strength.

"My mother would have done that," Fred said.

"She would have done what?" Elizabeth inquired.

"She would have prayed before she ate the orange. She has always asked the blessing at the table before we ate."

"Then you have a very good mother, Fred."

"Yes, I know that."

"Could we talk, Fred? Would you tell me something about yourself?"

"Like what?"

"Tell me about your family. Do you have brothers and sisters?"

"I have two brothers and one sister."

"What about your father? What kind of work does he do?"

"My father has always worked in the tobacco warehouses. So do my two brothers and my sister's husband."

"What about you, Fred, what kind of work are you in?"

"Do I look like I'm in any kind of work?"

"You are well spoken, Fred. Where did you get your education?" Elizabeth asked.

"I went to school and studied hard. I liked school, especially arithmetic and reading. I read everything I could get my hands on."

"Then what on earth has happened to bring you to this point in your life?"

"Well, Mrs. Bainbridge, it's like this, I have no intentions of going into the tobacco business and eke out a living. I figure there's more to life than that and an easier way to obtain it."

"You're making a dreadful mistake, Fred. Why don't you take me back home? My husband won't press charges against you. You can be on your way. Think of your family, especially your mother. What you're doing will break her heart. If you'll do the right thing now, you can avoid so much trouble in your young life. There are other things you can do without going to work in the tobacco warehouses. It's obvious you're smart and intelligent. If you apply yourself the sky can be the limit for you. Please Fred, take me home. My family is worried sick, I'm sure."

"You present a good case, Mrs. Bainbridge. But it's not that simple. I left my hometown about six months ago. I robbed a bank. That money is almost gone. I must have more. So you see, I can't go back."

"I can't see how you can do anything but go back. If you carry out this kidnapping plot, you'll be in real trouble with the law. If you take me home, then return to your home and confess to the bank robbery, you shouldn't have to serve too long of a sentence. But if you collect ransom money, leave here and are ever caught, you will serve a long time in prison. And, Fred, you can't hide forever. You will be caught. Then what kind of life will you have? Being free, even though you don't have the things in life you might like to have, is better than being imprisoned and having nothing. One last thing you need to think about, Fred. Jesus himself said, 'For what is a man profited, if he shall gain the whole world, and lose his own soul? Or what shall a man give in exchange for his soul?' If you continue on this path you'll not only lose your freedom but your soul." Elizabeth leaned forward in her chair to pat him on his shoulder, gently and with a motherly touch.

"You drive a hard bargain, lady, but enough of this kind of talk. Don't be fooled by our conversation tonight. I intend to carry through with my plan. You better get some sleep. I'll be watching you so don't get any ideas of trying to escape."

Chapter 34

Inspector Richardson had worked on this case until midnight. They needed daylight hours to search the outskirts of Richmond proper. By the time the merchants opened on Thursday morning the eleventh, officers were checking with them. None of them had seen a stranger in town over the last week. Some officers along with Vann, Albert, and several other men of the town had been sent to check the road between Willow Place and town. By noontime they had found nothing.

Inspector Richardson, in the mean time, had taken some officers to the carriage plant. They questioned workers, asking if they had seen anyone looking suspicious around the plant lately. They found no leads. Then they searched the grounds thoroughly. Inspector Richardson walked over to Luke's Livery Stable to question Luke Watson, the owner.

"Has anyone, not from around these parts, been in to rent a carriage lately, Luke?"

"Now that you've mentioned it, inspector, there was a new man in here yesterday afternoon. He rented a carriage about 3:00 and had it back by 4:30."

"Did you get his name?"

"Yes sir. I always take down the names of anyone who rents a carriage. It's right here on my ledger. He signed his own name. It's Joseph Landers. Mighty fine handwriting if you ask me," Luke declared.

"What did he look like?"

"Well, he was about five feet ten and weighed about a hundred sixty or seventy. He was dressed nice and very polite. He had dark hair with sideburns and a mustache."

"Do you usually notice people that well who come in here, Luke?"

"Yep, I do. They're taking off my property. I need to know what they look like in case they decide to keep on going."

"How old do you think he is?"

"Well, now, I'd say he's in his mid 20's."

"Did he act strange when he returned the carriage?"

"Come to think of it, he did act a little breathless and was in a big hurry to unhook his horse and get gone. He had a mighty fine horse too, an appaloosa."

"Which carriage did he rent from you, Luke?"

"This one right down here," Luke said, walking past three carriages to the fourth one.

Inspector Richardson gave a low whistle and said, "He surely chose a nice carriage to rent."

"Yep, he said he was going to pick up a lady and it had to be nice."

"Did he leave anything in the carriage when he returned it?"

"Well, yes, as a matter of fact he did, if I can find it. Here, let me look through the trash." He rummaged through an old can he was using to put trash in. "Here . . . yes, here it is."

He handed Inspector Richardson a dark piece of cloth about the size of a bandanna. It had a faint odor to it.

"Where did you find it, Luke?"

"It was on the floor of the carriage. He was in such a hurry he must have overlooked it."

"Thank you, Luke, you've been a big help. I want to take this cloth with me as well as your ledger he signed. I'll get the ledger back to you as soon as I can," Inspector Richardson said as he hurried out of the door.

"What's going on, I wonder?" Luke said to himself.

When Inspector Richardson arrived back at the station house, the men who had been searching the road toward Willow Place were coming in with dejected looks. Zachary was with them. Inspector Richardson called Zachary into his office after he asked the rest of the men to wait outside.

"Zachary, my man, I have some evidence here that just might help us catch this kidnapper."

They reasoned that Joseph Landers wasn't this man's real name, but the hand writing in the ledger and the ransom note was the same. The dark-colored cloth left in the rented carriage had been soaked in chloroform, so he must have used it to sedate Elizabeth. According to Luke, he was a clean and neat man who would not draw any particular attention to himself if he circulated around Richmond.

Inspector Richardson said he had to be living somewhere. They would need to check the five hotels in the area to see if someone meeting his description was staying at one of them.

"But inspector, we don't have that much time. It's already three o'clock. We only have until 6:00 this evening to meet his demands," Zachary lamented.

"Do you have the money ready that he's asked for, Zachary?"

"Yes, I had Mr. Page from the Richmond Bank to prepare it for me and hold it until I call for it."

"I'll call my officers together, give them the information we have and send them out immediately to these five hotels. Remember, the kidnapper asked you to leave the money under the oak tree on the south side of town. Well, you and I can go to the Jackson Hotel since it's on the south side of town. Let's see what we can find out. If we don't come up with a firm lead, then we'll have you take the money out to the tree and wait to see who picks it up. Agreed?"

"Alright, but I'll need to talk to Vann and Albert and tell them our plans."

Chapter 35

I'm sorry I had to shackle you to the bed again, Mrs. Bainbridge, but I had to have some sleep. You've kept your word not to scream. I'm going to untie you and let you freshen up a bit. Then I'll go and get us some coffee and pastries from the hotel dining room, Fred Stone said.

"You mean they have a dining room here? That surprises me," Elizabeth replied.

"They have a lot of people who stay here for months and a dining room is necessary."

After they had their breakfast Fred seemed to be getting nervous. He'd been in control up to this point.

"Do you think your husband will come through with the money I've asked for?"

"If you were in his shoes, would you pay the ransom money?" Elizabeth asked.

"Yes, I would if I had his wealth and if my wife were the victim," Fred replied.

"Fred, may I ask how old you are?"

"I'm twenty-two. Why do you ask?"

"I simply can't believe you're doing this to yourself," Elizabeth said.

"Aren't you concerned about what I'm doing to you? Do you realize that I've threatened your life if your husband doesn't give me the money I've demanded? Don't you think I'm serious?"

"Once again, Fred, I'm appealing to you. Please take me home before you do something you'll regret for the rest of your life. If you continue with this plan it will lead to your destruction. You can't win. But if you'll take me home before any ransom money is received, I can assure you my family will not press charges. And there is another scripture I feel compelled to share with you, 'For the wages of sin is death; but the gift of God is eternal life through Jesus Christ our Lord.' You need to think about this, dear boy."

"That's found in Romans 6:23, I ought to know, I've read it enough times. You remind me so much of my mother. I'd sure like to see her. She's a fine lady, my mother."

"Then why are you breaking her heart? That's exactly what you're doing, you know. Unless you've been a parent you can't know the love a father and mother has for a child. You can do the decent thing and turn your life around now, or you can go on being a thief and break her heart over and over again," Elizabeth said, wondering if what she said would anger him and push him in the wrong direction. But she felt she had to take that chance. Fred Stone was worth saving, she believed.

He hung his head and looked at the floor for a long time. Standing up, he began pacing, back and forth, back and forth.

He stood looking out the window for a time. Finally he turned and said, "I know what you've told me is right. I've really been thinking about going back to Lynchburg and facing what I've done for quite some time. This idea of kidnapping you for ransom seemed like an easy way out. But all this time I've known it was a horrible mistake. Will you forgive me, Mrs. Bainbridge?" Fred asked.

"Indeed, you are forgiven. What you've done has hurt you more than it's hurt me. It has also terrorized my family. I can only imagine the agony they've gone through. But during the time you've held me captive I've prayed for you, Fred. When you thought I was asleep I was praying silently for God to touch your heart and break the spirit that has had you bound. I have to believe that God has answered my prayer."

"I appreciate all the things you've said to me and the prayers you prayed for me. I'm not a stranger to God's word. I have been raised by God-fearing parents. There's no excuse for my behavior. I've let my desire for material things posses me rather than working to earn a decent living. I promise you I've learned from this experience. I'm ready to face the wrong I've done and pay for it. Thank you, Mrs. Bainbridge."

"Then we need for you to take me home quickly, Fred, before you're apprehended and charged. Once I'm home safely I'll get you some help."

They were riding double on Fred's horse toward Richmond when they saw two riders approaching. Elizabeth recognized Zachary and the inspector before they met. She told Fred to pull up and stop.

"Zachary! Oh Zachary, my darling!" Elizabeth exclaimed.

He looked startled, not being able to see Elizabeth for Fred, but he recognized her voice. Then she came into view.

"Elizabeth, is it really you? Are you alright?" Zachary said, as he jumped from his horse and reached up for her.

She literally fell from the horse into his arms and sobbed against his shoulder. "I'm fine. I assure you I'm fine. Seeing you released my pent up emotions, that's all."

About that time Inspector Richardson realized who Fred was. He ordered him to get down from the horse immediately. He began checking him to see if he had a weapon.

"Wait just a minute, Inspector Richardson. I want to talk with you and Zachary in private. Fred, go over and stand underneath that tree. It'll be alright. Trust me. Zachary, please may I talk with you two? Please!"

The two men didn't know what to think. But the urgency in Elizabeth's voice got their attention.

She explained the decision she and Fred had come to and filled them in about his predicament. It would take a long time to tell them the events of the last 24 hours. But she asked them both to please trust her judgment until they had time to talk further.

They walked back to where Fred was standing and he said, "I expect you to take me into custody, inspector. I'm ready to face the wrong that I've done and the consequences of my actions."

Chapter 36

The homecoming for Elizabeth was one of great joy and many tears of thankfulness. They all huddled in the parlor to listen to the story of her abduction. The Autry's, who had stayed with Savannah while her father and Vann were out searching, stayed to hear all that had happened. Elizabeth finished her story by appealing to all of them to try and understand Fred's dilemma. He was worth saving she honestly believed. The bank robbery was a very serious crime and he would have to take his punishment for it. But she asked the family not to bring charges against him for the kidnapping. She also asked Zachary to appeal to Inspector Richardson not to press charges against him. She realized that he could because, after all, he had taken her against her will, even though he did not collect a ransom.

"If we can show Fred a Christ-like spirit it could turn his life around. I feel it's worth a try," Elizabeth pleaded.

"We are so thankful to have you back unharmed. We'll abide by your wishes," Zachary assured her. "I'll go into town now and tell Inspector Richardson the whole story. The final outcome will be left up to him."

THURSDAY, SEPTEMBER 11ᵀᴴ, NEW YORK

Morgan paced back and forth at the train depot waiting for the Richmond bound train to arrive. He was devastated by his mother's kidnapping and anxious to be on his way home. Finally he heard the sound of the whistle and saw the billow of steam as the train approached the depot.

Settling into his seat he began to wonder what might have transpired since he received the telegram late yesterday. He simply couldn't let himself entertain the thought that his mother had been harmed. Instead, he began to think about his growing up years. He remembered the first slingshot he made. Getting pretty good at hitting any target he shot at, he decided to see if he could hit a bird. Sure enough he killed a red bird. Feeling very proud of himself, he picked it up and ran to his mother with prey in hand. He explained that it only took him one shot to hit it. Tears stung his eyes, even now, as he remembered her reaction. He could almost hear what she said to him then.

"Morgan, what have you done? This red bird probably has a nest of babies that depend on her to feed them. Without her they, too, will die. You are a very good marksman with your slingshot, but birds and animals should not be one of your targets. Please tell me you won't do this again. Now let's bury the little thing."

He remembered how she carefully wrapped the bird in a soft cloth and had him dig a hole. Together they laid it there, covered it over and marked the small grave with a stick cross. Then she drew him to her, held him very close and both of them cried.

What a tender heart she had. Always, always she was fair. She measured her punishment for his wrongdoings carefully. When the punishment was over, he knew he would always get a hug and an affirmation of her love for him.

Christmas was a favorite time for his mother. If it snowed she was absolutely elated. She especially loved sleigh rides.

It was their custom to shop on Christmas Eve. They bought gifts for families who were having a hard time. Surprising them with food, personal items and toys for the children was his mother's delight. On Christmas afternoons they always went caroling with their church group. His mother was a giver and a doer. Surely she would not be harmed by this person who had kidnapped her. He wondered what was going on at this very moment. Not knowing was the hardest.

The Chesapeake and Ohio rolled into the Richmond Train Depot exactly on schedule at 4:00 P.M. the next afternoon. Morgan was on his feet with his bag in hand before the train came to a stop. He was the first one off. To his surprise, there stood his beautiful mother with her arms outstretched to embrace him. He dropped his bag, ran to her and lifted her off her feet. Never had holding someone felt so good!

He, his father and mother hurried to Willow Place from the train depot. When they arrived it turned out to be a grand homecoming. Vann's family was all there as well as Phillip, Jane and Mary Ann Maxwell. As usual, when their family got together there were lots of hugs and kisses.

When Morgan saw Mary Ann he rushed to her, took her face in his hands, kissed her gently, held her in his big, strong arms and said, "You're going back to New York with me!"

Rosie had supervised a festive meal for everyone. It seemed more like Christmas than September 11th. When they finished eating they gathered in the library. All eyes were on Elizabeth and Zachary. It had only been a little over 24 hours since Elizabeth had been abducted, but it seemed like days. Morgan had really heard nothing of the ordeal and was anxious to know all the details. He spent the next couple of hours asking a lot of questions and listening to each detail as the story unfolded.

When the story of his mother's ordeal was finished, Morgan had a very thankful heart that she had been spared injury or even death at the hands of this man who so boldly abducted her. When he listened to how she had been gagged and tied, it stirred anger within him; however, when she finished the story of such a misguided young man as Fred Stone, he felt pity for the man.

"Mother, I have some things I want to say to you and father. I'd planned to tell you in private but feel that now is the time to bear my heart to you both." Glancing around the room at the faces of those so dear to his heart, he continued, "Please bear with me, dear ones, for a few minutes."

Morgan rose to his feet and walked across the room to the mantle. Standing there he could face his mother and father. He stood in silence for a few minutes, collecting his thoughts and quieting his pent-up emotions. Finally he began to speak.

"When I think of the verses of scripture that talk about love, joy, longsuffering, gentleness, goodness, faith . . . these attributes describe you, Mother, and you, Father. Your blessings have flowed to your children. Our lives are favored and blessed each day by the joy and pleasure we receive from you, the two most influential people in our lives. Father, you stand very tall in character and integrity. I can think of no other person I'd rather pattern my life after, and I love you very much."

Morgan stood still and reflective, looking at the floor. Finally he said, "Mother, these comments are just for you. When I received the news that you'd been kidnapped I can't tell you the despair that I felt. The helplessness of being so far away was maddening. As I traveled those miles on the train from New York to Richmond, I felt I could run faster than the train was moving. The scripture that tells us to pray without ceasing was ever on my mind. I found myself praying so fervently I was almost giving orders to our Heavenly Father! I also did a lot of thinking about you . . . about us.

"I am awed when I think of all the things your precious hands have done for me through the years. They caressed my face as a baby, brushed my curly, dark locks, fed me when I couldn't hold a spoon, tied the shoestrings of my shoes, comforted me when I was sad . . . just a few of the gestures of love I was too young to remember at the time.

"You placed wet cloths on my brow when I was sick, sat all night by my bedside smoothing the covers, making sure I stayed covered up. You held me in your arms, rocking me and singing to me when I had a bad dream, stroking my forehead until I fell into a peaceful sleep again.

"I remember many times sitting in church as I was growing up, comparing my hand to yours. There's just something so special about a mother's hands!

"I also remember the times you've read to me from the Bible, especially from the book of Proverbs. I practically know that book by heart! The time you spent with me has shaped my life in a very positive way. You and father have been a steadying influence in my life and your counsel has been an important part of my growth.

"In the last 24 hours I've never been more grateful for you as my mother. What I have said comes from the heart of a thankful son. I know how much you love 'your' song . . ." To Each His Own" Mom, and I'm so thankful you are my mother. I'm also thankful you are safely home here at your beloved Willow Place.

"One last thought . . . I remember reading this somewhere. 'Our family is like the branches of a tree. We may grow in different directions, yet our roots remain as one. Each of us will always be a part of the other.' I'm sure Savannah feels this very same way."

Morgan took a few steps and knelt at his mother's feet and said, "There now, I didn't mean to make you cry."

Elizabeth replied, "These are tears of joy, my son. My heart is overflowing with love and pride."

He stood to his feet and embraced his father and Savannah. This homecoming had turned into a time of great celebration rather than a time of sorrow that he feared it might be.

Chapter 37

Zachary had sent a telegram to the Bristol's as soon as they arrived back in town after finding Elizabeth and Fred Stone on the road south of town. But he sent them a more detailed message on Friday morning, September 12th. He knew they were anxious to know what was going on. The Bristol's had become a very important part of their lives.

He checked by the city jail with Inspector Richardson to see what decision he had made concerning Fred Stone. He learned that Fred had stolen $700.00 from the bank. Since Elizabeth felt so strongly that this young man was worth redeeming, he told the inspector he would send that amount of money to the bank in Lynchburg. And if necessary, Zachary told the inspector, he would go to Lynchburg to speak on behalf of Fred for clemency. They both decided that a letter from Zachary would be just as effective.

"What has made you and your wife so interested in this young man who has dealt you both such a low blow?" Inspector Richardson asked.

"Elizabeth did a lot of talking to Fred as well as a lot of listening to him. She has thought of his family and the pain they've already suffered, not knowing the whereabouts of their son and brother, much less the crime he had committed. She admits that she could be wrong about him. But if giving him a reprieve does turn him around, she says, what a victory it will be. Inspector Richardson, I did question her about all of this and she referred me to the scripture in Matthew where Jesus told his disciples, 'For the Son of man is come to seek and save that which was lost.' And she reminded me of the shepherd who left the 90 and 9 sheep to seek that one which was lost. She told me that we must do this for Fred Stone. This is just the way Elizabeth is. She has a most forgiving heart," Zachary said.

"This is a remarkable woman you're married to, Zachary. Yes indeed, a very remarkable woman."

Zachary went to the carriage plant to draft the letter for the inspector regarding Fred Stone. He checked with his foreman to see that everything was running smoothly, took the letter by the inspector's office along with a bank draft for the $700.00, then he returned home.

When he entered the house he found that there was an air of excitement. When he asked what was going on, he was told there was going to be a wedding!

Early Friday morning, while his father had gone into town to take care of business with the inspector, Morgan had asked Mary Ann to walk with him around the lake. When they came to the serpentine garden they sat on a bench facing the water.

"What a serene and tranquil place to be, Morgan. It's as if all is right with the world. It's a place where you can clear the cobwebs from your mind, don't you agree?" Mary Ann said, as she looked into Morgan's face.

"That's exactly why I brought you here this morning, Mary Ann. I have a very important question to ask you. Will you marry me Sunday and go back to New York as my wife?"

"My answer will surprise you, Morgan, perhaps. But, yes, I will."

"You mean you don't even have to think about it?" Morgan asked incredulously.

"No, my love, I don't even have to think about it," Mary Ann replied.

"Then perhaps you've already thought about it," Morgan said, with a knowing look on his face. "Is this right?"

"Yes, you're right."

"What may I ask brought this mindset about?" Morgan inquired, holding her small hand between his.

"Not to disparage what happened to Elizabeth, but if someone kidnapped me and I was never found then I would never get to be Mrs. Morgan Bainbridge! Seriously, Morgan, what happened to your mother made me realize how uncertain life really is. We should make every day count."

"Mary Ann Maxwell, you've stolen my speech! I was prepared to convince you of exactly what you've said to me. You've made it so easy! And you've made me so happy."

"You see the gazebo there on the north end of the lake? It was built just for a wedding. I don't think we should let it go to waste now, do you?" Mary Ann asked.

"Mary Ann, seriously, will you miss not having the excitement of preparing for a big wedding? I know how happy Savannah was in preparing for hers and Vann's wedding."

"No, Morgan, the most exciting thing is I will be your wife and can go back to New York with you. This happiness outweighs what you think I might be missing otherwise. Now, we've got a wedding to plan in just two days. We'd better get busy!"

"By the way, do I get a kiss from the bride-to-be?"

"I thought you'd never ask."

Entering the breakfast room where Elizabeth, Jane and Phillip and Savannah were having a second cup of coffee, Morgan cleared his throat rather noisily and said, "I hate to interrupt your conversation but time is of essence so I must. Phillip, I'm here to ask the hand of your daughter in marriage. Not in the distant future, but day after tomorrow."

It got so quite you could hear a pin drop. Phillip looked at Jane. They both looked at Elizabeth and then at Morgan and Mary Ann.

"Morgan, you know we have no objection to you marrying our daughter but what's the big rush?" Phillip asked, somewhat perplexed.

"I'll be going back to New York on Monday and I don't want to go without Mary Ann. She feels the same way. We both know this is a hasty decision but it's what we want to do," Morgan replied, almost apologetically. "Won't you please try to understand?"

"Mary Ann is our only daughter, Morgan. Her mother and I have always planned to give her a proper wedding when the time came. What do you think about this, Jane?" Phillip inquired.

"I'm inclined to agree with the children, Phillip. A large, formal wedding would give us all great pleasure, but circumstances make for changes. If this is what Mary Ann wants, then we should not stand in her way." Jane replied.

"Then it's settled. You have our blessings. Now, what can we do to help prepare for the ceremony?" Phillip asked.

"That's my father!" Mary Ann said, as she flung herself into his outstretched arms.

"Mother, what do you think of our plans?" Morgan asked, giving Elizabeth a warm hug.

"I couldn't be happier, Morgan. You know how your father and I feel about Mary Ann. Did my ordeal have anything to do with your quick decision?" Elizabeth inquired.

"It had everything to do with it. Life is too uncertain for Mary Ann and me to let another day go by without spending the rest of our lives together. You do understand, don't you?"

"We all understand," Elizabeth replied. "Mary Ann, just what do you have in mind for the ceremony? We'll do everything we can to see that you have a lovely wedding on Sunday."

Zachary arrived home from his trip to the inspector's office to find that wedding plans were in the making!

All the women got their heads together and by early afternoon on Friday, September 12th, plans were being made for the wedding to take place on Sunday afternoon at three o'clock.

Morgan and Mary Ann wanted the ceremony centered at the gazebo. The guest list would be very small, mostly family. Including the wedding party, there would be about thirty to attend. Morgan and Mary Ann picked up the marriage license and engaged Pastor Autry to perform the ceremony. They made the rounds telling the family about the hasty wedding plans.

Jane and Mary Ann shopped for just the right outfit. Elizabeth and Savannah got with Rosie and started the wheels turning for the reception.

Chapter 38

*S*unday morning, September 14th had started off with a very light rain, but by ten o'clock the sun came out in a cloudless sky. By noontime everything was dry and looked freshly washed. It was a perfect day for the three o'clock wedding.

Refreshment tables were set up in the serpentine garden area. The three-tiered wedding cake topped with sculptured wedding bells of butter icing graced one table. An heirloom silver punch bowl laden with fruit punch sat on another. Rosie had outdone herself preparing silver platters with assorted dainties for the guests. Heavy cut glass vases filled with a variety of garden flowers added just the right touch to the tables.

Savannah's piano had been placed next to the gazebo. Emily Autry, the pianist, as well as a violinist and flutist began playing as the guests were seated.

Heads turned to see Mary Ann approach the altar at the gazebo as the musicians played Wagner's Wedding March. She wore an ivory, silk brocade dress with fitted sleeves, a round lace collar at her neck and tiny satin-covered buttons down the front of the dress to the pointed waistline. The back of the dress was simple and featured a bustle with an overlay of lace matching the lace of her collar. She had chosen an elbow-length veil of ivory chiffon attached to a circular headband.

As her mother, Jane, watched her every move, tears filled her eyes and spilled over. Her tom-boyish little girl, who, like herself, could bait a fishhook as well as any old boy, looked exquisitely beautifully. Yes, she was all grown up now! A bigger lump filled her throat as she realized her little girl would be moving to New York far, far away.

As Phillip answered the question, "Who gives this woman to be married," he thought, *what am I saying? This is my child . . . she's not a woman! Morgan is taking her all the way to New York to live. This is much harder than I thought it would be.* But as he gave her a kiss, before he took his seat, he saw the look of radiant joy on her face and knew this was right for his Mary Ann.

Elizabeth looked at this handsome man at the altar, dressed in a black business suit with a white shirt, grey and black-striped ascot tie, and realized he was her baby boy all grown up. His strengths and weaknesses she knew well and knew of a certainty his strengths far outweighed his weaknesses. She knew Morgan would be a good provider for Mary Ann as well as her protector. She was very proud of her son and was elated that he and Mary Ann were pledging themselves to each other.

As Zachary looked upon this wedding scene his mind traveled back to his and Elizabeth's wedding day. It was very different than this but every bit as exciting. He saw himself in his son, the way he walked, the way he turned his head, and the gestures he made with his hands. He trusted Morgan to be a good and faithful husband to "little" Mary Ann. They already loved her like a daughter. He felt sad that Mary Ann's only brother, Greg, was not here for the wedding, but he had hired a sketch artist for Morgan's wedding just as he had for Savannah's. Greg could get a feel of what it was like from the sketches.

Savannah, who was the matron of honor, and Vann, who was Morgan's best man, looked at each other during the ceremony and remembered that four months ago they were saying their vows in exactly the same place. It brought back many memories. Savannah loved her brother very much and Mary Ann was already a kindred spirit. Today was a happy day at Willow Place.

Right on cue the white horse and carriage appeared with JUST MARRIED written on the back. Mr. and Mrs. Morgan Bainbridge stepped inside and the driver took them up the hill to the 'Morgan' house. The sound of applause followed them until the carriage was out of sight. Vann and Savannah were staying the night with her parents, Elizabeth and Zachary. They had prepared a guest room for the newlyweds. The next morning they would be catching the train to New York to begin their life together.

Chapter 39

OCTOBER 11, 1881

Zachary was standing on the front porch drinking some spiced cinnamon tea, one of his favorite hot drinks, on this Saturday afternoon. He was admiring the exquisite blaze of color on the mountain area overlooking the west side of the lake. Joseph's coat of many colors, mentioned in the Bible, could not have been more beautiful. He found the fall of the year to be very invigorating. His attention was drawn to the driveway where a carriage was approaching. It was a carriage from Luke's Livery Stable and it stopped in front of the steps. A man and woman, whom he had never seen before, stepped down from the carriage.

"Are you Mr. Zachary Bainbridge?" asked the man.

"Yes, I am."

"Please excuse our intrusion but may we speak with you?"

"Of course, won't you come inside?" Zachary said, stepping aside and gesturing toward the door.

Zachary showed them into the library. The man said, "My name is Andrew Stone. This is my wife, Martha. Our son is Fred Stone. Could we please speak with your wife also?"

Zachary asked them to be seated and rang for Rosie. He asked her to have Elizabeth join them in the library. His curiosity was certainly piqued by this unexpected visit.

As Elizabeth entered the room Mr. Stone rose to his feet immediately. Zachary introduced the Stones to Elizabeth, who greeted them warmly.

Zachary inquired, "What has brought you all the way from Lynchburg to our home?" as he motioned to Mr. Stone to be seated again.

"We come to you with great embarrassment. We cannot explain our son, Freddie's, deplorable violation of you folks. His mother, his brothers, his sister and I are at a loss as to why he resorted to bank robbery and kidnapping. Your graciousness to him in this matter is beyond our comprehension. We are humbly grateful to you for your mercy."

Martha sat with her head bowed and wiped the tears that slipped down her face unchecked.

"Your generosity in sending back the stolen $700.00 to the bank was really unthinkable after what he put your family through. We have come today to return the money. Freddie's brothers and I combined our resources so that we could do this. We must do this," Andrew said emphatically, as he counted the money and laid it on the end table next to the chair where he was sitting.

Zachary and Elizabeth looked at each other in amazement. This confirmed to Elizabeth they had done the right thing where young Fred Stone was concerned. What a difficult task this was for his parents. However, it proved that Fred Stone came from good stock as her 'Dandy' Baldwin used to say.

"Tell us something about your son, Mrs. Stone. Why would he have even considered robbing a bank?" Elizabeth asked.

"Well, you see, we've always banked with Mr. Davenport at the Lynchburg bank. He was as shocked as we were to learn that Freddie took money from his bank. Freddie worked at the bank after he graduated from high school. He's a very smart boy, good in arithmetic. He did some bookwork for Mr. Davenport on a part time basis. Then he went to work in an attorney's office full time. We thought he was headed in the right direction. We were very proud of him," Martha said, but with the saddest look in her eyes.

"What action has been taken against him?" Zachary inquired.

Andrew answered, "When Inspector Richardson brought him back to Lynchburg, Freddie said he was guilty of robbing the bank and wanted to take his punishment for the crime. After a consultation between Inspector Richardson, Mr. Davenport, the banker, and our Inspector Hawkins, they decided to take the case before the judge. Because Mr. Davenport wanted special consideration for Freddie, he was sentenced to five years, two-and-a-half to be served in confinement and the other two-and-a-half on probation. God in His mercy smiled favorably on our son in this matter," Andrew said thankfully. "Since you and Mrs. Bainbridge did not personally press charges against Freddie for kidnapping, your Inspector Richardson chose not to bring charges against him either.

In fact, no one in Lynchburg knows about what he did here in Richmond. We owe you folks for this," Andrew said, quite visibly touched.

"I can assure you, Mr. Stone, I was not as quick to forgive your son as my wife was. She pleaded with me on his behalf. I didn't feel kindly toward a man who would take my wife from the safety of her yard, chloroform her, gag her, shackle her to a bed and keep her prisoner over night, and all because he wanted money and the good life without working for it. But Mrs. Bainbridge was touched by his youth and felt sympathy for you, his parents. She counseled with him and saw a redemptive quality there. This is why I agreed to help Fred. Since meeting the two of you I'm thankful we chose to do so. I believe our trust in him will be rewarded. For your sake, I hope so," Zachary declared.

By this time Mrs. Stone sat with her head bowed and her hands lying loosely in her lap. Elizabeth thought her heart would break for this troubled mother. She walked over to Martha and embraced her warmly. Mr. Stone stood to his feet and said they must leave.

"Where are you going?" Elizabeth asked.

"We have a room for the night in Richmond and will be catching the early train in the morning for Lynchburg. We would have come to you before now, but we had to wait until we saved the money to repay you the $700.00. This is a very embarrassing time for us, but it was something we had to do. You've been gracious to receive us into your home. We can never really repay you for what you did for our son," Andrew said.

Elizabeth asked, "Will you please give Freddie a message for me? Tell him to study every chance he gets while he's in prison. He needs to stretch his mind, taking this opportunity to do so. When he's released and serves his probation time, he can be prepared to turn his life around completely. If there's anything we can do to help him at that time we will do so."

Zachary extended his hand to Mr. Stone and agreed with what Elizabeth said about helping Fred.

Elizabeth gave Martha a hug and told her to put the past behind her. "Look to Jesus, the author and finisher of our faith. He will help you and your family. Please let us hear from you. If Fred will write to me I will answer his letters."

After the Stones left, Elizabeth wept for them, feeling so helpless in this matter. Zachary said he didn't want to accept the money they had brought, but felt he must do so for their self-esteem. He told Elizabeth he was going to stay in touch with Inspector Hawkins in Lynchburg and check on Fred's progress. He assured her they would do what they could to help this family.

Chapter 40

OCTOBER 16, 1881

Elizabeth hurriedly opened the letter from Morgan and Mary Ann. This was the third letter she had received from them since they went to New York. It was dated October 10th. She began reading . . .

Dearest Mother and Father,

We have just gotten moved into our brand new home. It really isn't new but it's new to us! We're so excited. Mary Ann has made some sketches of both the outside and inside to give you an idea of what it looks like.

Mother, Uncle Jordan and Aunt Hannah have been so good to us. Uncle Jordan has given me a pay increase. Aunt Hannah has donated some furnishings she had stored away. We're ready and waiting on visits from home! We now have room to entertain house guests. Please consider coming to

New York for Christmas this year. Bring Savannah and Vann with you. Mary Ann will ask her parents to come also.

Mother and Father, we will be forever grateful for the beautiful wedding you and Mary Ann's parents provided for us there at Willow Place. We built memories on "our day", September 14, 1881; memories that will be forever etched in our hearts.

We have loved your letters. Please keep them coming. Most of all, we love you two precious parents. Give our warmest regards to Savannah and Vann. Tell them they owe us a letter!

With our love,
Morgan and Mary Ann

Letters from the children were always welcome and read many times over. They would be making a trip to New York for Christmas this year for sure, but not just to see Morgan and Mary Ann. The Bristol's had also invited all of them for the holidays, including Phillip and Jane.

After supper Zachary and Elizabeth went into the parlor and curled up on the sofa in front of a crackling fire. As parents so often do, they spoke of the joy their children had brought to them, recalling the day they were born and their growing up years.

"Remember the Saturday afternoon, Elizabeth, when we had just finished giving Morgan and Savannah their baths before their nap time and somehow Savannah slipped out of the house without a stitch of clothes on?"

"Remember? How could I forget? While you were drying Morgan off, I had to rush outside and chase Savannah down. I caught her just before she got to the stables. She insisted she was going to ride the pony!" Elizabeth said with a chuckle.

"Then there was the time Morgan caught the garden snake and hid it in his pocket until bedtime. He planned to let it sleep with him. Remember when you went to tuck him in and help him say his prayers? You found him sound asleep and the snake was curled up on his chest. You screamed such a blood-curdling scream it could have wakened the dead. Then it took an hour for all of us to calm down and remind Morgan that snakes don't live in the house with people!" Zachary said, laughing at the memory.

"They're all grown up now and have begun a journey of their own. I pray God that we have successfully trained them for this journey," Elizabeth said.

"And I too, Elizabeth. There are a lot of crooks and turns in life. But with God's help we've made it thus far, and I believe Morgan and Savannah have the tools and the Godly training to do the same. My heart swells with pride when I think of our children."

"One month from today will be November 16th, our 25th wedding anniversary," Elizabeth said, as she slipped a little closer into the circle of his arms. "I've been thinking about how we might celebrate it. Do you have any ideas?"

"Most importantly, I want you to be pleased. It should be a very special celebration," Zachary replied.

"Savannah has already said she wants to plan a big party for us. But Zachary, I don't want a big party. I feel exactly as I did about our marriage. I'd like to 'elope' all over again! I'd rather celebrate this anniversary just the two of us. How do you feel about it?"

"Do you really want to know? Let's do it. Let's elope all over again! We'll tell Savannah we have plans of our own. Agreed?"

"Agreed!" Elizabeth echoed.

At the breakfast table the next morning Zachary asked Elizabeth how she would like to take the train to St. Louis. He reminded her how they had met at the train depot and began their journey together on a train. They had not traveled west at all and it should be an exciting adventure.

Elizabeth loved the idea. She felt like a bride all over again. Looking at Zachary across the table from her, she thought how young he looked. His head full of hair was as blonde as ever. Few wrinkles lined his face. His eyes were still as blue as the sky and the charm of his smile melted her heart. There was such a special magic just being in his presence. She had a great desire to give back to him all the special love she had received. His very touch caused her heart to leap boundlessly. In her heart of hearts she felt no other couple had ever experienced the depths of love they had.

"There's that look again that I love so much. I see your heart in the pools of those very gorgeous eyes," Zachary said, reaching across the table to clasp her hand. "What were you thinking about?"

"What was I thinking? I was thinking of the dreams we've made together and how so many of them have come true . . . so much so that I feel I'm walking ankle deep in stardust. Our memories are like our dreams. They belong to us to share only as we see fit, and they tell our story, our very own personal and private story. As I've told you so often, my love for you is boundless," Elizabeth said tenderly.

"Are you trying to 'tease' me into staying out of work today, my dear?"

"No, my sweet Zachary, I was just answering your question," Elizabeth replied, mischievously.

Chapter 41

Sunday, October 19th

Elizabeth thought the choir sounded like angels singing in the Sunday morning service. No matter how many times they sang "Amazing Grace" it always sounded new and fresh to her.

Pastor Autry read from Second Corinthians chapter 12, verses 7 through 10 of the Apostle Paul's writings.

7. "And lest I should be exalted above measure through the abundance of the revelations, there was given to me a thorn in the flesh, the messenger of Satan to buffet me, lest I should be exalted above measure.

8. For this thing I besought the Lord thrice, that it might depart from me.

9. And he said unto me, My grace is sufficient
    for thee: for my strength is made perfect in
    weakness. Most gladly therefore will I rather
    glory in my infirmities, that the power of Christ
    may rest upon me.

10. Therefore I take pleasure in infirmities, in
    reproaches, in necessities, in persecutions,
    in distresses for Christ's sake: for when I am
    weak, then am I strong."

Pastor Autry preached a stirring message on these passages of scripture. He emphasized the ninth verse . . . "My grace is sufficient for thee."

Elizabeth and Zachary left the service feeling refreshed and grateful for God's amazing grace.

The Bainbridge family was gathered around the dining room table at Robert and Rebecca Thomas' country home for an early Thanksgiving gathering. It was the best time for most of them to be present. Rebecca Bainbridge Thomas and her husband, Robert, had become prosperous farmers in Richmond. Zachary and Rebecca's parents, Steve and Barbara Bainbridge who lived in Williamsburg, had come for a week's visit. Their brothers Ben, his wife, Andrea, and Thomas and his wife, Joyce, also from Williamsburg, had accompanied their parents for the visit.

Elizabeth looked at the faces of this dear family she had married into. She remembered when she first met them. What a rock of Gibraltar, her father-in-law, Steve was. He had been steadfast in his convictions, always, and his actions portrayed his convictions. He and Barbara were in their early seventies but were still very active. Their home had always been a safe and loving environment, very nurturing to their children.

After the meal was finished they moved into the large living room and gathered around the piano to sing and listen to Barbara, an accomplished pianist. Savannah adored her Grandmother Barbara. She watched every move her talented fingers made on the piano keyboard. All had agreed that Savannah inherited her natural ability to play from her grandmother.

Zachary was especially happy to have his family all together. He and Rebecca saw each other on a weekly basis since they both lived in Richmond, but he didn't get to be with the rest of his family as often as he would have liked. He sat quietly and listened to the talk and laughter that surrounded him. They shared many stories that had happened since they were together last. Then they reminisced about their growing-up years and roared with laughter at some of their antics. The brothers did a lot of sparring with words and teased Rebecca unmercifully as they did in their youth. She loved every minute of it.

The week passed quickly and was filled with long talks and lazy evenings before the fire, more reminiscing and many gatherings around a table full of food. When those visiting left on the train for Williamsburg, they all agreed they would make this an annual event.

Chapter 42

WEDNESDAY, OCTOBER 22ND.

Zachary heard a light tap on his office door at the carriage plant. He looked up from the plans spread over his desk of the newest carriage design and said, "Come in."

He was surprised to see Vann as he opened the door and stepped inside. "I'm sorry to barge in on you like this," Vann apologized, "but there's a matter I need to discuss with you."

"You're always welcome anytime, Vann. How can I help you?"

"I'm glad you put it like that because it's help that I need. You might not be aware of the fact that Savannah has been a true friend to Kate Miller and her husband, Luke, ever since she had the accident on the ridge when she went to tutor their son, Adam."

"Yes, I'm aware that Savannah has stayed in touch with them, and I'm glad."

"I ran into Luke yesterday at Ingram's Hardware Store. He was buying some tarpaper and shingle nails. We talked for a few minutes. He said their house, if you can call it that, was leaking badly. He was sick with a terrible cold. I told Savannah about our encounter and neither one of us could sleep last night," Vann said with a sigh.

"I remember that Luke was a tremendous help when Savannah was lost and injured so seriously," Zachary interjected.

"Savannah has found out that they are very fine people, Zachary. Luke and Kate have been looking after an elderly, invalid neighbor who has no family. His wife worked tirelessly tending to him, and growing what they ate. She actually did the work of a man. She died about three years ago."

"You say the man is an invalid. What caused this, or do you know?" Zachary asked.

"Savannah said Kate told her he had a stroke a year before his wife died. It left him paralyzed on his right side. He was able to sit up and managed to get from the bed to the table and back but that was it. They were a very devoted couple with no children. They actually had two children early in their marriage, but each died shortly after they were born," Vann said, shaking his head.

"Luke and Kate are very unselfish people to be so involved with non-kin in such a personal way," Zachary declared. "Not many people would be so generous with their time."

"Luke's parents both died in a house fire when he was just fourteen, so he felt somewhat drawn to this couple. Due to the responsibilities they feel for this neighbor, which requires a lot of his time, Luke and Kate make do by raising their own food, selling what they can from Luke's wagon and picking up odd jobs. Kate is a good seamstress and takes in sewing when she can get the work. Luke knew the old man could not live very long and he simply could not abandon him. As it turned out, he lived much longer than expected. But he died three weeks ago."

"What are their plans now, do you suppose?" Zachary asked.

"Kate told Savannah Luke is a very good horseman and has a natural ability in working with horses. He now wants to get a better job and a better place to live for his family. There's no reason for them to stay where they are any longer."

"It sounds to me like we need to see what we can do to help this family," Zachary replied. "Do you have something definite in mind, Vann?"

"Yes, as a matter of fact I do. I've spoken with my father about this and he's in total agreement. We have a piece of land to the south of our place that we could put a house on. Savannah and I would like to have a 'house-raising' for the Miller's. Father says everyone at the horse farm can all pitch in to help. Do you think you could spare the men that work for you at Willow Place to lend a hand?" Vann asked hopefully.

"That would be no problem. What about the lumber and materials it would take to do a job like this?" Zachary asked.

"Father and I will go in together and buy the materials. If Luke will go along with this plan, he can go to work for us at the horse farm and make payments on the cost of the materials. When it is paid for the house will be his. They're really fine people. It seems the odds have just been against them ever getting off that place where they now live. If we can give them a leg up I feel they can be very productive citizens of our community. Building the house with donated labor will be the secret to its success. What do you think?" Vann asked.

"It's a great idea, Vann. A great idea! Not only will I pay my employees right on while they're working on this project, but I'll make a donation toward the material expense," Zachary said.

"I knew you would help. We need to get started on the project before the weather turns bad. I'm going to talk with Luke and see if he's willing to go along with this plan. I should know something by mid afternoon. I'll get back with you," Vann said as he shook Zachary's hand.

"In the meantime, Vann, I'll contact a contractor to give us some direction on this project."

Chapter 43

On Friday a crew of fifteen men was on hand to dig the foundation for the Miller house. There were lots of strong backs in this group. As the days went by it was almost like magic to watch the progress being made on the 'house-raising.' There seemed to be a strong spirit of giving among these men. It was surprising at the talent and skills apparent among the workers. The contractor that Zachary spoke to furnished plans for the project and came by daily to keep the men on the right course. The unity manifested was almost a spiritual thing.

Savannah was ecstatic about the project. She and her mother had gone through things they had packed away to help furnish the house when it was completed. One room in the 'Morgan' home (that's what Vann and Savannah continued to call the house even though it now belonged to them) was filled with extra furnishings that had belonged to Savannah's great grandparents, John and Catherine Morgan. These were nice things and had been stored carefully.

Savannah knew how much Kate loved pretty things and what good care she took of all she had. Elizabeth was reminded of the way she, herself, felt when she was helping the Everett family. She was thankful to see that Savannah had the same spirit of wanting to do for others. Vann had asked Luke not to tell Kate and Adam about the house so that it could be a complete surprise for them. The weather had cooperated. They had only one day of rain so far, and it came after they had the roof on the house.

The Miller house was to be just a country-style home. The floor plan called for three bedrooms on one side of a long hall, with a large kitchen, dining room and living room on the other side. There was to be a water closet at the end of the hall. This is something the Miller's had never had before.

The building contractor had become so interested in this 'house-raising' project that he decided to have three of his best men come and spend a week working on the inside doing the finish work. He was a Christian gentleman. He said that he couldn't lose by lending a helping hand to this fine family.

Savannah had seen the furnishings the Miller's had in their home from going to help Adam with his studies when he had the measles. They had a four-room house very sparsely furnished with a mixture of odds and ends. If Vann would have let her, Savannah would have taken her furniture and put it in the Miller's new house! She wanted things to be perfect for them.

With the house almost completed, Savannah and Elizabeth were doing an inventory of the furnishings they had gathered to determine what was lacking.

"Mother, Vann says they have an extra bed in the bunk house with a good mattress that we can put in Adam's room. Remember the old desk that Morgan used as a little boy and

216

finally discarded? Do you know what happened to it?" Savannah asked.

"Yes, Savannah, it's stored in the stable and has been for many years now."

"Do you think we could ask Albert to clean it up so that we could put it in Adam's room?"

"That's a good idea, Savannah. It's small and will fit nicely. The chair that went with it is also in the stable."

"There's a washstand in my pantry with three drawers. I can certainly do without it. As a matter of fact, it's really been in the way. We can put it in his room. With fresh curtains and a couple of blankets for the bed his room will be complete. Oh, Mother, I am so excited about this," Savannah said as she gave her mother a big hug.

With all the help the house was finished in record time. Wednesday, November 12th, the house was ready for occupancy. Everyone who had a part in this concerted effort was present when Luke, Adam and Kate rode up in their wagon. Luke climbed down from the driver's seat and walked around to the side where Kate sat. He reached up to help her down. She looked at all the people and at the house. She hesitated, not wanting to step down out of the wagon.

"What are we doing here, Luke? Who are all these people? We have no business being here. This is not like you," Kate said under her breath.

About that time Vann and Savannah stepped out from among the crowd and walked to the wagon. A hush came over the crowd. Vann reached up to Kate and asked her to step down. Then he lifted seven-year old Adam out of the wagon. Next, he climbed up into the back of the wagon, using it as a platform, and began to speak.

"Kate, we're all gathered here today for a special reason. Really it's a celebration, a celebration of Christian love and care for some very special and deserving people. Look around you, Kate, all these people here today are here to present you, Luke and Adam with a key to your new house. That's right, your new house. These 20 plus people are the ones who have built this house by the sweat of their brow. They've done this unselfish deed because they knew you had a need. Luke will be working for Baker's Horse Farm and will pay for the materials it has taken to build it. The labor, however, is a gift. Here is the key to the front door. We hope you like it."

The crowd began to clap and cheer. Kate swayed so that Luke had to hold her up. She kept repeating, "I can't believe this. I can't believe this," as they threaded their way through the crowd.

They stopped when they stepped up on the front porch. Luke turned to face the people. "I'm at a loss for words to adequately thank you for what you've done for me and my family. This is such a big thing. Such generosity is hard to comprehend. But I can assure you that anytime there's a need in the community, I'll be the first in line to lend a hand. We want to be contributors and somehow try to make up to all of you kind people for what you've done for us. From the depth of our hearts we thank you."

Luke felt a tugging on his coattail. Looking down, he saw Adam's upturned face and heard him say, almost in a whisper, "Father, are we going to live in this house?"

By this time Luke was completely overcome with emotion. He stooped down and held his little boy close and began to weep. Everyone in the crowd was wiping their eyes and blowing their noses, including the big, tough cowhand they all called "Stormy."

Vann spoke up and said, "Luke, I think you should carry your wife over the threshold of her new home."

Everyone began to clap and chant, "Katie, Katie, Katie!"

When they entered the house a roaring fire was going in the fireplace and the cook stove. The dining room table, from Catherine Morgan's stash, was laden with all kinds of food. By this time Kate was all smiles and was exclaiming over the fairytale that was unfolding before her very eyes.

After a tour of the house everyone gathered in the dining room and Pastor David Autry was asked to bless the food.

"Our loving and giving heavenly Father, it is only fitting that we should quote the words at this gathering that you spoke to your disciples in the book of Luke. 'Give and it shall be given to you; good measure, pressed down, and shaken together, and running over, shall men give into your bosom. For with the same measure that ye mete withal it shall be measured to you again.' Lord, we feel that these dear ones who have given so freely of themselves to build this house will certainly reap a bumper crop. It is with thankful hearts that we receive this feast of food that is set before us. And, oh Lord, bless the hands that prepared each morsel. Amen."

The fellowship among all the people was genuine and without pretension.

When the people said their goodbyes and the front door closed, Luke held Kate in the circle of his arms and said, "Can you believe this, Kate? Can you believe this is our home?"

Tears had welled up inside Kate all afternoon but she stifled the urge to let them surface. Now, finally, she gave over to great sobs that shook her entire body. They were tears of joy for sure, but floods of tears, nevertheless. Her heart was just overflowing with gratitude.

Adam had done some exploring on his own. He exclaimed over the water closet as he pulled the chain that released the water into the toilet bowl. After his second pull on the chain, he was reminded by his father that it wasn't a toy!

Adam went his room and found a toy train and some books on his very own desk. He sat down on the bunk bed that Vann had personally made up with blankets just like in the bunkhouse at the horse farm. He looked up on the wall where Vann had arranged a small pony saddle, a brand new cowboy hat, a lasso and a pair of small spurs hanging from wooden spikes. Underneath was a low wooden bench with a colorful saddle blanket draped over one end.

He looked up at his mother and said, "It looks like I'll be working at the Baker's Horse Farm just like my father. They must think I'm a really big boy."

After Adam was bedded down for the night, Luke and Kate sat in front of the large fireplace watching the burning embers of the extra big log, too excited to even think about sleep. Luke explained to Kate how all this came about. She had walked through this rustic but beautiful home from room to room, touching things but not believing all of this was theirs. The house was not full of furniture but there was enough to do them for a long time to come. Of course they would have to go back to the old place and pick up some personal items, but the majority of it would be left for the next renter. Also, they knew they would have to make payments on this house. Luke's new job working for Mr. Chuck Baker on the horse farm was a Godsend. He would show them they had not misplaced their trust in him.

Luke looked at Kate curled up beside him on this wonderful sofa and realized just how pretty she was. The daily grind of late had kept him from noticing her as he used to. She had kept that lean, trim figure and had taken care of her personal grooming. Her fresh, natural beauty set her apart, and her long, dark hair and olive skin made her look like an Indian maiden, especially, he thought, with those dark brown eyes that reminded him of a sweet baby doe. She could do the work of a man but never lost that feminine air. She did what she did with great ease and without complaining. He felt very humbled as he realized how blessed he was to have her love.

Kate looked with wonder at this ruggedly handsome man sitting beside her. What great strength of character he possessed. He was so gentle and kind. He treated every living creature with kindness. Not once had he ever raised his voice to her or Adam. He believed in discipline, both self discipline as well as discipline in the home, but he did it with great fairness. He would have been a wonderful teacher as he lived his life by example, even his caring for Mr. Brown, their neighbor. They just sort of inherited him after his wife died some three years ago. But Luke said they had to care for him because he had no one else. Luke was an avid reader, was self-educated and especially liked poetry. He made her feel like a princess when he told her of his love for her. She felt a great prayer of thanksgiving fill her heart because she was loved by such a man as Luke Miller.

Chapter 44

Savannah was curled up close to Vann in bed, her head resting on his shoulder. "Wasn't today one of the most exciting and fulfilling days you've ever spent? I'm still too excited to sleep. Did you see the look on Kate's face when Luke carried her through the door and the surprise when she first entered their bedroom? Mother and I did a pretty good job coordinating their room, don't you think? Do you reckon Luke liked it? You're a man. What do you think? The extra bedroom was a little bit lacking, don't you think? But at least we were able to have a bed, dresser and chair for it. Did you like the quilt we used on the bed for a spread? And what about . . ."

"Savannah, Savannah, my love, slow down just a little bit. You're full of questions but are not waiting for answers! All that's been done has been worth it just to see your reaction and your enthusiasm for doing good things for others. You're certainly happiest when you're giving. I've never been more proud of you nor loved you more than right now. You and

Elizabeth took an empty house and filled it with so much personality, and you accomplished it with things we already had. Your creativity was very apparent to everyone. I watched as you, knowing Kate, tried to visualize what you thought she would want and the way she would want things arranged. You and Elizabeth poured yourselves into this wonderful project. I'm sure Kate recognized this. You'll have a chance to talk with her and hear her comments about it all. And Savannah, you'll have another dear friend close by. I myself am looking forward to working with Luke at the farm," Vann said, hugging Savannah just a little tighter.

"Vann, Adam's room was a delight for that dear little boy. You fixed it just right. His eyes sparkled all afternoon. Did you notice how he looked at you? I saw him trying to mimic the way you walked and the way you stood. I also saw you kneeling down and talking with him. What did you tell him?"

"I told him he could spend lots of time with us at the horse farm and that we had a pony just waiting for him to ride. I asked him if he liked his room that is almost exactly like mine when I was a small boy. Then I told him that he and I were going to be big buddies."

Savannah and Vann talked into the wee hours of the morning. They agreed they would never forget November 12, 1881.

As Elizabeth and Zachary prepared for bed, Elizabeth asked, "Have you ever been more proud of Savannah and Vann than you were today?"

"I can't say that I have. We've always known how giving Savannah is but Vann showed us during this project that they are a perfect match. He's a fine young man indeed," Zachary answered as he watched Elizabeth brush her long, black, curly hair, a nightly ritual.

"What happened these past three weeks was certainly a fulfillment of the commandment 'Do unto others as you would have others do unto you.' Did you listen to the words of Pastor Autry's prayer when he asked God's blessing over the food, using the words of Jesus about giving? You know, Zachary, I don't wonder at the Lord telling his disciples, 'Man shall not live by bread alone, but by every word that proceedeth out of the mouth of God.' His word is our strength," Elizabeth said as she laid her brush down and turned from the mirror.

"We've spoken about the day's events, my sweet Elizabeth. Now let's get a good night's sleep as we've got lots to do to get ready for our 'elopement!'"

Looking up at Zachary from the circle of his arms, she asked, "Am I your girl?"

"You always have been!" Zachary answered as he pressed his warm lips tenderly to hers.

Chapter 45

THURSDAY, NOVEMBER 13, 1881

Elizabeth and Zachary had discussed where they wanted to go for their anniversary trip. St. Louis, which would be a three-day and three-night train trip one way, was at the top of their list. A new train terminal had been built in St. Louis called Union Station. It housed a large hotel with many gift shops and restaurants plus a theater. This was very appealing to them. Secondly, they had considered going to New York but were going there for Christmas, which was only a month away. Thirdly, they thought about retracing their steps the day they were married, which they did on their tenth anniversary. So they finally settled on the St. Louis trip. They were as excited as two young people on their first date.

Their trunk and bags were all packed. Elizabeth wrote Savannah a letter explaining their plans and left it with Rosie to give to her the next day.

Elizabeth was excited about what she was wearing for the trip. She had found a dark green velvet dress made very similar to the one she wore the first time she met Zachary twenty-six years ago and also wore on their elopement day twenty-five years ago, the one he loved so much! A form-fitting green wool coat, almost identical to the coat she wore that day, was a part of the ensemble. She could not believe it when she saw the outfit in the window of Picketts in downtown Richmond. She knew she had to have it.

When she emerged from the dressing room, Zachary was standing with his back to her looking out the door to the balcony. The moonbeams were threading their way over the lake making shimmering patterns of light from one side to the other. The willow trees' outlines could be seen in the moonlight.

He was wearing a dark business suit. She stood looking at his broad shoulders and slim hips, admiring this man who seemed to have changed very little in the past twenty-five years.

Sensing her presence he turned around. She was focused on his face to get his reaction to what she was wearing. He literally gasped at her image and was speechless for a few seconds. Then, with a twinkle in his eyes, he said, "You must be Miss Elizabeth Sloan."

She quickly answered, "And you must be Mr. Zachary Bainbridge."

He lifted his top coat from the bed, reached for a brand new yellow scarf lying beneath it, wrapped it around his neck, slipped on his top coat and replied, "Yes . . . yes, I am."

They knew immediately this was going to be a trip of a lifetime!

Albert had all their baggage loaded into the carriage. They gave last-minute instructions to Rosie and stepped out into the moonlight and up into the carriage. Their train to begin their anniversary journey west was leaving at 9:05 P.M. When they arrived at the train depot, Albert unloaded their baggage on the loading dock while Elizabeth stayed seated in the carriage. Zachary made his way inside the larger, more modern waiting room and walked to "their" window, standing where he had stood twenty-six years ago when he first laid eyes on Elizabeth. When Elizabeth saw his face she stepped down from the carriage. She looked all around the platform, just as she had done twenty-six years ago, then she proceeded to walk slowly toward the door.

Zachary caught his breath again at her loveliness. She was the same size she had been that day long ago. Her hair was still as black as raven's feathers and her perfect widow's peak gave her face the shape of a heart. Wearing the deep green dress and green wool coat, buttoned snugly which accented her tiny waist, made Zachary feel as though the clock had been turned back in time to November 16, 1855. Moving toward the door of the train station, she looked like a dream walking. As the door opened Zachary turned around. He involuntarily thought, just as he did twenty-six years ago, would she notice that he was wearing a yellow scarf?

Elizabeth stepped inside the door, stopped and looked around the room. She was looking for a man wearing a yellow scarf. Her eyes stopped on the man standing near the window. He was the most handsome gentleman she'd ever seen . . . and was wearing a yellow scarf just like John Lee Morgan had said . . . twenty-six years ago!

He had silvery blonde hair and a great physique. He was a little over six feet tall and still had that glorious tan that comes from sailing. Drawing near to him she looked into those familiar eyes that were as blue as the sky on a cloudless day. She felt breathless and a little dizzy as though this moment had been frozen in time.

She extended her hand and said, "You must be Zachary Bainbridge," her mouth spreading into a warm and familiar smile.

He thought *how can one be so perfect?* He particularly noticed her violet blue eyes, long eyelashes and perfectly shaped eyebrows. Her engaging smile revealing deep dimples in each cheek made her look invitingly impish, a look he was so familiar with.

He said, "Yes, I'm Zachary Bainbridge." He reached for her hand, leaned over, kissed it and then said, "You, my dear, are Elizabeth Sloan Morgan Bainbridge and you are mine!"

The bench they sat on 'back then' had been replaced with a longer one having padded leather seats and backs, divided with wooden arm rests. They sat where they could see the train as it approached.

"Eloping" like this for their twenty-fifth wedding anniversary put Elizabeth in a very festive mood. What a grand event to be celebrating, twenty-five years as man and wife! She realized that a good life is really built on hope, and faith strengthens that hope. When it is seasoned with love it makes for a very rich life indeed.

Zachary leaned very close to Elizabeth and whispered, "I hear there is a train due in here any minute heading for St. Louis. Will you run away with me, fair lady?"

"My dear man, what would your wife say?" she replied, as they heard the approaching train's whistle.

Chapter 46

They were seated in the third passenger car on the Atlantic & Pacific. It was very plush with comfortable seats. The passengers in the car were a friendly group. There was a distinguished looking white-haired gentleman sitting across the aisle from them. He was dressed in a suit with western-cut boots and a dark Stetson perched on his knee. He was on the train when it arrived in Richmond. When they took their seats he nodded and spoke very cordially.

"When Rosie gives my letter to Savannah I wonder what she and Vann will think about us leaving on our trip without telling them," Elizabeth asked.

"I'm sure they'll think it's wonderful. It just might give them some ideas about their anniversaries in the future," Zachary replied with a smile.

They sat close together so their conversation could be private and reminisced about some of the sweeter moments in their lives. They said some very intimate things to each other, intended for their ears only. They were so engrossed in their own world they were unaware of the time. Soon they noticed they were about the only passengers left in their car. Realizing it was very late and they needed to retire for the night, Zachary motioned for a porter to show them to their Pullman car.

Elizabeth had chosen a very dainty, white nightgown. The front yoke was embroidered with soft pastel flowers. The long gathered sleeves had ruffles at the wrist with the same embroidered trim. Her black hair framed her face as she lay on the pillow. Zachary marveled at her beauty and even more at her inner beauty. He slipped in between the sheets, gathered her in his strong arms and, holding her gently, whispered his love for her, kissing her tenderly several times. Zachary and Elizabeth savored this special world their love transported them to, a world their very own. They believed it was a place no other had ever entered. It was their private utopia filled with unspeakable bliss. Elizabeth knew theirs was a very special love. Finally, the rhythm and sound of the train moving over the tracks lulled them to sleep.

Breakfast time found them making their way to the dining car. Their waiter reminded them of the one who served them on their wedding morning when they eloped and left Richmond for Williamsburg aboard the Chesapeake & Ohio. That waiter was an older black man who did things with flair, as did this man. They both had the right personality for the job.

Zachary noticed that the older white-haired man in the western suit was sitting just across the aisle from their table. Again he nodded to them.

When they returned to the passenger car they looked out the window at the passing scenery. The fall of the year had come late and there were still colorful leaves on the trees in this mountain range. The brilliant morning sun shined on the trees highlighting the vibrant reds, glistening golds, flaming oranges, and shades of green and brown in a kaleidoscope of radiant colors. They were absolutely awestruck by what they saw.

Elizabeth was like a child, exclaiming over first this scene and then that one. The older gentleman laughed at her exuberance. He asked if they were from Richmond since that is where they boarded the train. They began to exchange conversation. The seat directly in front of them was unoccupied. He asked if he might sit there and did so at their invitation.

The gentleman introduced himself as Kirk Walker from St. Louis. He said he owned a cattle ranch there. He had been visiting a brother in Williamsburg and was on his way back home.

Zachary extended his hand to the man and said, "I'm Zachary Bainbridge and this is my wife Elizabeth."

"Would you be the Bainbridge that owns the carriage company in Richmond?" Mr. Walker asked.

"Indeed I am. How do you know about Bainbridge Carriage Company?"

"From one of your former employees, Max Hammond."

"And how do you know Max?" Zachary inquired.

"I met this very energetic young man eight years ago when he first came to St. Louis. In fact, he came to work for me at the Circle K. My wife, Vivian, and I were never blessed with children so we've kind of adopted Max and Jo Anna and their three sons. He has never compromised my confidence in him and has risen to the top at the Circle K like cream does on milk."

"You know, I thought your name sounded familiar when you introduced yourself. My sister, Rebecca, is married to Jo Anna's brother, Robert Thomas. Jo Anna is in touch with her family by mail. She, Max, and the boys have been back for a few visits after they left Richmond and moved to St. Louis. I recall them speaking of the Circle K and its owner Mr. Walker. It seems this kind of work is what Max is cut out to do. Oh, he was happy all right in the carriage work. But he decided he needed a greater challenge and felt he could find it by going west. I think he's a true 'cowboy' at heart," Zachary said with conviction.

"Not only is he a true cowboy, but he's a leader as well. He didn't mind starting at the bottom, taking his licks as they came without complaining. He stayed with a job until it was completed no matter how long it took. When he began to advance at the Circle K there was no animosity against him. He has the utmost respect of those who work under him. When Max is in charge I don't have to worry. It was a good day for us when he came to work at Circle K. Viv, my wife, sure loves that family," Kirk Walker said with a smile.

"You are blessed to have Max working for you. I certainly hated to lose him from the carriage plant. He made things happen there. I completely understand your description of Max," Zachary added. "It's quite accurate."

"What brings you two to St. Louis, except to visit Max and family, may I ask?" Mr. Walker inquired.

"This is a very special event in mine and Elizabeth's life. We are celebrating our twenty-fifth wedding anniversary by taking this trip to St. Louis. We have read about Union Station and decided we wanted to see it firsthand. Our visit with Max and family will be a surprise," Zachary said.

"May I offer my heartiest congratulations! Vivian and I celebrated our thirty-sixth anniversary last June. Our journey together has been a good one."

"Have you lived in St. Louis very long, Mr. Walker?" Elizabeth inquired.

"We've lived there 30 of those 36 years. I inherited my land from an uncle and we decided to raise cattle. We started out small but with perseverance and very hard work we've built the Circle K into quite a spread."

"Maybe we can see the Circle K when we visit Max and Jo Anna," Zachary said.

"Elizabeth, do you two have children?" Mr. Walker asked.

"Indeed we do. We have a son, Morgan, and a daughter, Savannah. They are both married."

They spent several hours exchanging information about their families.

Chapter 47

Saturday, November 15th, was a rainy day. In the early morning there was an abundance of fog. Visibility through the train windows was not good so they were unable to see the scenery they were passing. However, there was a spirit of merriment inside their passenger car. After traveling together for two days passengers were mixing and mingling, getting to know one another.

One young man was traveling with a banjo. He felt comfortable enough now to take it from its case and began to play a toe-tapping tune. This got the attention of everyone. When he had finished there were shouts of, "More! More!"

He surprised everyone by playing and singing "I Dream of Jeanie with the Light Brown Hair" by Stephen Foster. His tenor rendition had a nostalgic yearning to it, almost as if he were singing about a certain young lady. The passengers would not let him stop. This was much-needed entertainment and diversion from the dreary day outside. He had them all join in singing the catchy songs, "Camp Town Races" and "Way Down

Upon the Suwannee River." While singing his last song, he got up from his seat and walked down the aisle near where Zachary and Elizabeth were sitting. Stopping before a young lady sitting alone, he began playing and singing, "Oh! Susanna."

The young lady had been traveling alone on the trip. This young singer must have noticed. When he finished the song, to a hearty round of applause, he sat down beside her and engaged in conversation. The romantic part of Elizabeth thought . . . *now this could be interesting!*

That evening for their dinner meal Elizabeth noticed that the young couple was eating together. She also noticed he had brought his banjo with him. After they had finished their meal, he took the banjo out of the case and the two of them walked to the end of the dining car. He propped his foot on an empty seat and rested the banjo on his knee. Again he began to sing, "I dream of Jeanie with the Light Brown Hair," but this time she joined him. Their harmony was unbelievable. It was as if they had always sung together.

When they finished he announced, "I'm Chandler Crawford." Turning to the young lady he said, "This song bird is Robin Fowler. We discovered we are both headed for a job at the Terminal Hotel in Union Station as singers. What a coincidence that we should meet. If you like what you hear, you can hear more if you stay over at the Terminal Hotel."

They received a great round of applause. Zachary and Elizabeth smiled at each other knowing they would most likely hear them again.

Sunday morning, November 16, 1881, dawned with a blue sky and marvelous sunshine. They would arrive in St. Louis at 2:30 in the afternoon. The train trip had been a great experience for Elizabeth and Zachary. They had met and talked with many interesting people and were convinced that people were very much alike. Everyone had joy and pain in their lives. People needed an ear to listen. They heard funny stories, sad stories, intriguing ones and happy ones as they intermingled with the other passengers.

They, too, had shared some special stories of their lives with these friends and especially about their beloved Willow Place. Everyone they talked with showed an interest in the recent "house-raising" they had for the Luke Miller family.

The train whistle sounded as they neared the St. Louis Union Station. The passengers were busy exchanging addresses and bidding one another farewell. Elizabeth and Zachary talked with Kirk Walker asking directions to the Circle K. He had invited them out on Tuesday, November 18th to see Max and Jo Anna. He would send a carriage to the hotel for them.

An article had appeared in the Richmond Daily News some months earlier about the St. Louis Union Station. It had caught Zachary's eye and he pointed it out to Elizabeth saying they must visit there sometime in the future. The article included pictures, but they were anxious to see it with their own eyes.

The article mentioned that Union Station was designed by German-born architect Theodore C. Link of St. Louis. It said, "The architecture is a mix of Romanesque tradition and Norman style. It is modeled after a walled medieval city in Southern France with its sweeping archways, detailing fresco and gold leaf design, and exudes a very romantic flavor." Zachary knew this would catch Elizabeth's eye!

They were not prepared; however, for what they saw when they arrived. They had read that the train shed covered 11 acres and soared 140 feet in the air. But viewing it was an awesome experience.

Upon entering the building, neither were they prepared for the grandeur they beheld. It had 65-foot barrel-vaulted ceilings in the Grand Hall, all Victorian with a stained glass Allegorical Window positioned above the Station's main entrance. The floors were highly polished hardwood with huge space rugs here and there. Elizabeth exclaimed over the color scheme of rust, brown, deep tans, blues and greens that was used throughout the complex. It was very rich looking. The lighting was also very good. Gaslights on posts were spaced along the wide expanse of the interior of the building. The train terminal was to the left and was a huge area. It was filled with people who were traveling. To the right were many boutiques. At the far end was the Terminal Hotel.

It was good to be off the moving train and be able to walk at will. Zachary made arrangements to have their luggage carried to the Terminal Hotel where they would be staying. Then they walked through some of the boutiques. There were so many unique things to see that Elizabeth forgot about being tired from the trip. She made some mental notes of things she wanted to purchase before they returned home. She wanted something special to carry back with her as a memento of their twenty-fifth anniversary. Finally, they decided to go to their room and freshen up for dinner.

When they were given the key it was room number 116. Elizabeth, with her quick mind noted that the first two numbers represent the month of November, their wedding month, the second two numbers represent the day they were married! She liked this. The room, too, was beyond their expectations. It looked like a bridal suite! And why not . . . this was their anniversary. The rosewood bed had tall, carved, bedposts and was spread with a cotton silk comforter in a shade of ecru. The wall behind the bed was polished rosewood, with celery green paint on the other three walls, accented with rosewood cornices. A sofa of plush, dark blue velvet and a matching chair graced one side of the spacious room. There was a round table of rosewood with two matching chairs for an in-room meal. The dresser and chifforobe completed the furnishings. This was going to be a comfortable stay at the Terminal Hotel.

Chapter 48

After Zachary freshened up he excused himself to locate the Fred Harvey Restaurant in the hotel. He located the manager, Mr. Harvey, and explained he and his wife had come to St. Louis and the Terminal Hotel to celebrate their twenty-fifth wedding anniversary. They needed reservations for the evening meal. Zachary asked for a table near the entertainment area, but still as secluded as possible. He had secretly packed the white bud vase and white linen napkin with a red rosebud embroidered in one corner. He asked Mr. Harvey to place the vase in the center of their table with the napkin tucked inside so that the red rosebud showed. Then he gave him the note he had written to Elizabeth on their honeymoon at the beach house in Williamsburg twenty-five years ago. He asked that it be placed where Elizabeth would be sitting. Mr. Harvey was very cooperative and smiled broadly, telling Zachary he would see that his wishes were carried out to the letter. Zachary made it well worth his time.

Elizabeth dressed very carefully for "their" anniversary dinner. Her hair was piled high on top of her head with the curly tendrils framing her face just the way Zachary liked her to wear it. She had brought a violet blue-fitted dress with a banded neckline edged in same color lace with long fitted sleeves and a fashionable bustle and a gored hemline. Zachary had given Elizabeth a blue sapphire pin edged in lacy silver for their twenty-fifth anniversary that she had pinned to the band of the neckline accenting the beauty of the dress. Standing back, looking in the full length mirror, turning first this way and then that, she was pleased with what she saw and hoped Zachary would like her selection for this special occasion.

She heard this low whistle and turned to see Zachary watching her. He was impeccably dressed in a black dinner jacket, fitted trousers, a ruffled fronted white shirt and an ascot tie with a handsome silver stickpin which Elizabeth had given him. His perfect tan, blonde hair, with just a touch of grey in his sideburns, and that ever so charming smile melted her heart. He walked to the mirror, stood beside her and said, "Do you think we'll pass inspection?"

She answered, "Let's just say we've done the best we can," and gave him an impromptu kiss.

Walking to their table in the spacious dining room, heads turned as they passed by. Elizabeth noticed they had a strolling ensemble of violins and a trumpet playing 'falling in love' type music.

She was still looking all about as Zachary pulled her chair out for her to be seated. When she was comfortable she looked at the table. Zachary was watching her intently. She looked and then raised her glance quickly to meet his. Again she looked down at the table, staring for ever so long, finally catch-

244

ing her breath. When she raised her eyes they were glistening with unshed tears.

"You remembered. After these many years, you remembered your tribute to me on our honeymoon at the beach house. And you brought it with you just for tonight. Zachary, my very own Zachary," she whispered as she lifted the note from the table and read to him what they called their personal love note from the great writer and poet, Johann Wolfgang von Goethe.

This is the true measure of love . . .
When we believe that we alone can love . . .
That no one could ever have loved so before us . . .
And that no one will ever love in the same way after us.

"We have that true measure of love, Zachary."

"Those words describe perfectly the way I feel about the love we share," Zachary said as he reached for her hand. "On this earth you are the only person who has seen into the private places of my heart."

She picked up the bud vase with the somewhat yellowed napkin tucked inside, exposing the red embroidered rosebud and tenderly outlined the rose with her fingertip. Never had she felt her love run any deeper for this wonderful man than at this moment.

It was then the strollers appeared at their table and began to play their song, "To Each His Own." Zachary looked at her knowingly. She knew that he had arranged this. When the strollers finished, they bowed and moved away as quickly as they came.

Elizabeth and Zachary had a delicious meal served by one of the impeccably dressed waitresses known as the Harvey girls. The conversation over the meal centered on reliving their honeymoon. They still felt young at heart as in 'those days,' but had the measure of maturity only years of experience could bring. As they looked into each other's eyes the very air seemed charged with electricity. They didn't need words at this time. The things they felt for each other poured from their eyes into each other's hearts.

Drinking their third cup of coffee they heard the sound of a banjo. They saw movement on a small stage in their peripheral vision. Low and behold there was the young couple from the train, Chandler Crawford and Robin Fowler. They sang the haunting words of "I Dream of Jeannie With the Light Brown Hair" and did it beautifully. This was an unexpected delight to finish up their evening meal.

They strolled through some of the shops on the way back to their room. In a very fine boutique called The Specialty Shop they found a small silver bell engraved with two swans. They bought it as a memento of their twenty-fifth anniversary night and had the words "Forever Yours" engraved on the backside of the bell with the date and their initials. Zachary reminded Elizabeth that swans mate forever!

Elizabeth had already dressed for bed and was busy brushing her hair. Zachary was standing in front of the lusciously warm radiator watching her. When she laid the brush down he felt a little mischievous. She stood up and turned around right into his arms. He suddenly began tickling her in her ribs. She squealed in delight, pulling away from him and racing around the room, eluding his grasp as she went. They wound up falling on the bed. Zachary tickled her until she gasped for breath. They laughed and laughed just as they did on their honeymoon night.

Sliding in between the satiny feeling sheets, Elizabeth cuddled up close to him. She breathed a deep sigh of contentment and asked, "Zachary, am I your girl?"

"You always have been."

"Will you always take care of me?"

"Always, my love, always."

Continuing a long-time routine, but ever so sincere, Elizabeth said, "Tell me, Zachary, how much do you love me?"

"Why, I love you a whole sky full! How much do you love me, Elizabeth?"

"There's no height high enough, no depth deep enough, no width wide enough, and no words fine enough to measure my love for you, Zachary. But I'll have the rest of our lives together to show you."

"Will you seal that with a kiss?" he asked as he lifted her face and kissed her tenderly.

Long after Zachary was breathing the sleep of contentment Elizabeth lay curled up close to him. She couldn't seem to "turn off her mind" tonight. She thought of so many times she had thrilled to the sight of Zachary walking toward her in a crowd, but it was as if he were the only person there. She remembered how the very touch of his hand caused her heart to sing. She could see the tilt of his head when he looked down at her with that special smile. She remembered the times she had stifled the desire to exclaim to the whole room, "He's mine. He belongs to me!"

The beauty and thrill of it is, after twenty-five years, we still share those same intense feelings for one another, she thought. Zachary told her many times that their marriage is a rare one.

She thought young love is wonderful, exciting, sharing and learning. But mature love is wonderful, exciting, sharing and knowing . . . knowing one another, even knowing what the other one was thinking so much of the time without even having to ask . . . knowing the good and the bad, but loving and accepting just the same. Ours is a full-grown love, Elizabeth thought, just before dropping off into a contented sleep.

Chapter 49

Monday was filled with shopping and exploring this magnificent building. The article they had read in the Richmond News about Union Station didn't tell the half of its beauty. They made some purchases for Savannah and Vann as well as Morgan and Mary Ann. Going back to Harvey's Restaurant for lunch, they were delighted to be entertained by that winsome pair, Chandler and Robin and his banjo. It seems Mr. Harvey realized just what a talent these two had singing together and was taking advantage of it.

Tuesday morning, November 18th, Kirk Walker had personally come for them in his carriage. They were on their way to a surprise visit with Max and Jo Anna Hammond. Zachary was inspecting the carriage with his eyes, something he couldn't help doing in any carriage in which he rode. Not bad, he thought, not bad at all.

When they arrived at the Circle K it was evident it was a working ranch. A lot of activity was going on. An expanse of countryside was fenced with Black Angus cattle roaming the range. There were men in the distance repairing the barbed-wire fence. Another group was repairing a barn. Several cowhands were examining cattle in a corral for injuries or parasites. A very experienced rider was breaking in a mustang at another corral. This activity was very fascinating to Zachary and Elizabeth.

Kirk ushered them into the house to meet his wife, Viv. She was of slender build with a blonde plait wrapped around her head. Her skin was peaches-and-cream perfect. She had natural beauty that needed no help. What a striking couple she and Kirk made.

Extending her hand to Zachary, she said, "Welcome to the Circle K. You don't seem like a stranger as we've heard so much about you from Max."

She had a warm, firm handshake just like Kirk.

She stepped around Zachary and reached for Elizabeth, giving her a warm hug and said, "Jo Anna has told us so much about you two. You're so welcome in our home."

The family room was spacious with an open beam ceiling. One wall was lined with well-stocked bookshelves. Another wall had the biggest open fireplace Elizabeth had ever seen with a sprawling, red brick hearth and mahogany mantle that matched the beams. The roaring fire gave off enough heat for the entire room. Aztec influence was very evident in the décor of the room. Elizabeth loved it.

They were served piping-hot spiced tea with fresh-from-the-oven pound cake. The Walkers were so easy to be with. After an hour's visit they felt almost akin to them.

There was a knock at the door. Kirk had asked Max, Jo Anna and their boys, Thomas, Andrew and Joseph, to come for lunch that day. Little did they know Zachary and Elizabeth were there. They were in for a great surprise.

Zachary was standing when they entered the big room. Thomas saw him first. He exclaimed, "Uncle Zack, what are you doing here?" Then he saw Elizabeth and made a beeline for her. "Aunt Liz, what a surprise! You're still as purty as a speckled pup."

Thomas was more like his father, Max. He was full of fun and a big teaser. He labeled Elizabeth with the name 'Aunt Liz' from the time he could talk. Now he was 18 and all grown up.

Andrew and Joseph gave her a big hug after greeting their 'Uncle Zack' as they also called him.

Max and Jo Anna were ecstatic to see family. They inquired about Robert and Rebecca and the rest of Jo Anna's family back in Richmond.

Zachary and Elizabeth were surprised to see how much the boys had grown. Andrew was 17 and Joseph 16. They were truly what one would call 'stair-steps.' This kind of life had been good for them. The three were brown as ginger cakes and hard as steel.

In the early afternoon Max, Jo Anna, and the boys took Uncle Zack and Aunt Liz to their house that was on the Walker property and furnished for them by Kirk. It was evident that Kirk and Vivian had done well in the ranching business, brought about by hard work, good management and dedicated ranch hands.

They saddled up a couple of horses for Zachary and Elizabeth. Kirk and Max wanted them to see some of the things they did on a working ranch. Their barns were very impressive. They watched as horses were being broken in at one coral. The smithy was busy shoeing horses and had gotten a little behind. Thomas slipped on a heavy leather apron and surprised Zachary and Elizabeth with his skills in horse shoeing.

A cow had gotten caught in the barbed wire in the north pasture and was cut pretty badly. The boys worked quickly and expertly to get her untangled. Max had some disinfectant in his saddlebag for just such an occasion. They applied some of it to the cuts, slapped the cow on its behind and away she went.

They were shown through a couple of the bunkhouses and the main dining room where all their hands ate. It was a much bigger operation than Zachary had ever imagined. He had a greater respect for ranching after their tour.

That evening they all had a wonderful meal back up at the Walker's place. Afterward the Hammond family entertained them playing stringed instruments and singing. This family was something else! The boys had all taken after their parents and could they ever harmonize. This had been icing on the cake for Zachary and Elizabeth. Max had not lost a bit of his sense of humor. Jo Anna was adored by her boys!

Riding back to the hotel Elizabeth was glad that she had worn a wool poncho over her heavy coat. This St. Louis weather was a mite colder than they had in Richmond in November.

On Saturday night before they were leaving to go back home on Sunday, they had invited the Walker's and the Hammond's to have supper with them at Fred Harvey's Restaurant. They learned that Mr. Harvey, the Walker's and Hammond's were good friends. There had been a Cattlemen's Association meeting in St. Louis held at the Union Station. Mr. Harvey had provided their meals for them. During the last night of the meeting, Mr. Harvey had the Hammond family to entertain during the banquet meal. Kirk related this story to Elizabeth and Zachary.

Mr. Harvey approached their table when he saw they were through with their meal and asked the Hammond's to sing and play a few numbers for the restaurant guests. Elizabeth was completely taken aback by their talent on stage. It was one thing to sing in the comfort of a friend's sitting room, but to perform in front of a live audience was another. They were in rare form and their relaxed personalities wooed the crowd. They were good, very good. Knowing it was Elizabeth and Zachary's favorite song, they ended with Max and Jo Anna singing "To Each His Own" in perfect harmony. It was a wonderful way to end an already perfect evening.

They said their goodbyes and asked that the Hammond's and the Walker's all travel back to Richmond in the near future.

At eight o'clock sharp the next morning the train left Union Station heading back to Richmond. Zachary and Elizabeth had a lot of reliving of the last week to do. It had been a glorious anniversary trip, even greater than their anticipation! The time they had spent with Max, Jo Anna and the boys was one of the highlights of the trip.

As they traveled through the state of West Virginia Elizabeth couldn't help but hear the words of Stephen Foster's "Carry Me Back to Old Virginia" resounding through her mind. She loved traveling, going different places, seeing God's creation, but she was always the happiest to get back home to her beloved Richmond and Willow Place. She knew she was a southerner at heart and always would be.

Chapter 50

April 30, 1882

Elizabeth had heard the saying all of her life that April showers bring May flowers. She found it to be very true. Willow Place was dazzling with color, from the pink and white dogwood blossoms to the yellow forsythia bushes, clusters of jonquils, tulips and a variety of other flowers. Accenting these colors were the weeping willow trees in their "skirts" of deep green.

Zachary had taken the day off to be with Elizabeth. She had awakened in a very nostalgic and romantic mood and persuaded him to spend the day with her. She didn't have to do much persuading, not this gorgeous lady who was the love of his life.

They were having muffins and coffee on the balcony outside their bedroom, basking in the beauty that surrounded them. The birds were singing almost as if their songs were orchestrated. The wind was calm so the waters of the lake were very still. The two white swans swam lazily. What a picture to behold, Zachary thought. Living twenty-five years in this setting did not dim its beauty and enchantment to Zachary. He turned his eyes back to the person who had introduced him to this utopia they called home. She did not know how adored she really was.

"What made you awaken in such a nostalgic mood, Elizabeth?" Zachary inquired.

"I dreamed about our wedding night and it brought back a flood of memories. But instead of being at the beach house, I thought we were here at Willow Place. The dream was so intense that when I woke up I wasn't sure I'd been dreaming. My heart was pounding with the love I felt for you. I simply knew I had to spend the day with you," Elizabeth replied.

"Could you be more specific about your dream?"

"I saw my reflection in the mirror as I was brushing my hair and your reflection as you watched me. I relived the excitement of walking into your arms and being held as Mrs. Zachary Bainbridge. Then I was ushered into our very own world with you that no one else has ever been to. The dream was so real. Zachary, I'm so blessed that I pledged my troth, my fidelity, my continuing faithfulness to you and you alone," Elizabeth replied as she began to cry.

"Why are you crying, Elizabeth?"

"Because you know I always cry when we talk seriously about each other. I'm so touched and stirred that our love is so strong, so binding, my very own Zachary."

"Our life together has been one of commitment, not only to each other but to our beliefs about life. I know we have based our beliefs on a firm foundation so that when the storms came we were not washed away. And the storms did come! Life is like that. But we have had the glue to hold us together. Going back to the first time I ever saw you . . . you came sweeping into my heart, stole it completely and have never given it back," Zachary said, as he traced her lips with his fingertip.

"Zachary, are you happy I was so insistent on living here at Willow Place? Have you ever felt I was selfish in my insistence?"

"Truthfully, at first, I wasn't sure of my feelings about this place. However, I certainly knew what your feelings were. You made it clear there would be no compromise. My concern was that I make us a good living. I know that I have done that so I have no regrets. Willow Place is like no other place I've ever seen anywhere, anytime. Willow Place is you . . . Willow Place is me . . . Willow Place is us."

The End

To order additional copies of

Have your credit card ready and call:

1-877-421-READ (7323)

or please visit our web site at
www.pleasantword.com

Also available at:
www.amazon.com
and
www.barnesandnoble.com

Printed in the United States
43858LVS00005B/76-99